PITFALL

MARK SUTTON

PITFALL

Book One:

Pitfall:
Heaven's First War

By
Mark Sutton

Printed in the United States of America

Published by Hope Again Books

An Imprint of LifeFilters, LLC

Book Cover Design by ebooklaunch.com

Cover Illustration by Emily Jiang and adapted by ebooklaunch.com

❋ Created with Vellum

To my wonderful angels: Nancy, Amy, Jennifer, Rick, and Sarah.
And to the angels in their lives: Alexandra, Josh, Kristyn, and Jeremiah.
Thank you for the joy you bring to Donna and me every day.

CHAPTER ONE

"So . . . hard," panted the cherubim as it struggled through the Mists of Light. The smaller version of the angels realized, too late, its wings were unsuited to this part of Heaven. Energy depleted from fighting the gusting, rainbow currents that buffeted its body, wings failing, the cherubim was also unaware of the danger ahead or of the angel far above.

"If I can just make it . . . a little farther." The fragile being strained to gain the relative safety of space just past those mists. There, huge cliffs came together, forming a corner that served as a barrier to the swirling currents.

Above, the watching angel could see a tall, thin figure flying from the opposite direction. His jerky motions revealed a clumsiness that could prove deadly at this height. The angel watched the collision prepare to take place far below -- and his vast powers could do nothing to stop it.

"Oh!" The flyer shuddered as he bumped into the cliff walls and fell hundreds of feet. With much difficulty, he caught himself, remounted to the former altitude and continued on. His goal this time, the corner where the mists began, lay just ahead. He increased his pace.

"Watch out!" the angel called out to the cherubim in a loud

voice. "Someone is coming from the other direction!" His lips thinned in disgust as the noise from the powerful mists caught his words and carried them away from the two below.

A moment later, his worst fears were realized. A gust of light current shot the cherubim forward at great speed. The tall, thin flyer angled up suddenly, buoyed by an updraft. Two bodies slammed into one another, neither prepared for the impact. A sickening crunch reached the angel's ears, and he watched as the two stunned bodies began to lose altitude and fall toward the rocks beneath the mists. He folded his wings back and, with a sigh, dove toward the two. There was little chance he'd be able to catch them.

The cherubim and the flyer continued to fall. Their bodies picked up speed, tumbling end-over-end as they passed into the first part of the Mists of Light. The angel knew those mists hid sharp rocks of varying height. Heedless of the danger, however, he continued to accelerate. His speed now made him look like a streak of lightning aiming for sure destruction. Long golden hair streamed out behind him, resembling a third wing. Huge muscles strained for ever more speed. Angelic eyes tried to pierce the mists. It would be close.

Then he got a break.

"Wha . . . what's happening?" The flyer regained consciousness!

"Grab the cherubim beside you and fly away!" commanded the angel.

His speed was such that the clumsy flyer couldn't stop his fall. But he saw the angel rushing to his aid and did what he could to slow the rate of descent by flaring his wings and grabbing hold of the cherubim.

The angel could feel the rocks rushing up to meet them. With a last, desperate lunge, he grabbed both beings in his arms and then aimed himself *at the rocks*!

"What are you doing?" The flyer choked on his words. Fear rose in his throat like a bitter lump. He'd been rescued, only to see himself in danger of smashing against the rocks at an even greater speed than before.

The angel remained silent. All his concentration focused on the rock in front of him. At the last instant, he managed to swerve to the side. He passed so close to the rock's surface that the left side of one wing raked across the edge.

"Unh," he grunted, grimacing with the effort.

The deliberate collision had its intended effect, however. It swung him around, away from the other rocks and toward open space. He spread his wings and climbed toward the top of the cliffs, looking for a place the three could rest.

The angel found a flat surface and laid the cherubim and flyer on the ground. "Give me a moment to see what kind of damage I did to myself." He checked his wing for injuries. "Not too bad," he noted. "It'll heal soon enough."

A look of satisfaction crossed his face as he examined the two he'd rescued. The possibility of crashing into the rocks himself had been worth it.

"Is . . . is the cherubim going to be okay?" The flyer cast a worried glance at the small creature still lying unconscious on the edge of the great cliff.

"Everyone's going to be fine," replied the angel. He gently picked up the cherubim and stroked its forehead for a moment with one wing. "You can wake up now, little one. The trouble is over," he murmured. Heaven's smallest being moaned as its eyes began to flutter, then open. The cherubim looked around, unsure of where it was.

"What happened?" it asked.

"You and Volthra'an had a collision," the angel explained. "Both of you need to be more careful when you fly."

The being in question turned toward the other two as he heard his name. "I . . . I'm sorry. I shouldn't have been in this section of Heaven. I only wanted to practice -- to get better in my flying."

"Volthra'an, there's nothing wrong with practicing," his

rescuer said. "But did Michael give you permission to come into this area? After all, it's harder to fly here than anywhere else in all the Eternal Country."

The thin, clumsy flyer shook his head no. He kept it bowed, ashamed to look the golden, long-haired angel in the face. "I'll try to be more careful from now on," he whispered.

Satisfied that the two were okay, the angel spread his huge wings and began to lift off. "Had you hit them, those rocks would have caused you to be grounded for many light cycles," he called back to the recovering flyer and cherubim. "I suggest neither of you fly in the mists any more unless it's necessary."

Before either being could respond, their rescuer climbed ever higher. Golden hair flowed behind the angel, reflecting the River of Light.

———

Heaven. God's Home. The Eternal Country.

By whatever name its inhabitants used to describe their surroundings, all would agree on one thing: light dominated everywhere, liquid light carried by a vast river so ancient no creature could remember a time when it had not united all of Heaven.

Only divine eyes could withstand the intensity of the pulsating River of Light. Anyone gliding above it, following it as the light made its way through Heaven's vast country, would discover the river so illuminated everything and everyone that no shadow existed.

Flowing throughout the farthest reaches of Heaven, bestowing a divine glow of radiance upon everyone it passes, illuminating vistas of stunning beauty, the River of Light eventually slows and moves into an enormous plain. Unhindered now, the light folds in upon itself, growing deeper, vaster. As it expands, that which had been a river seems to grow restive. Bubbling and churning, the pool begins shooting streams of light high into the air. Faster, farther fly the light streams until, in a stunning display of God's power, the river finally follows, forging a path straight up into space, climbing hundreds of thousands of feet above Heaven's surface. There it pools, a deep, brilliant ocean of divine light visible to all the inhabitants of Heaven, a liquid sun proclaiming the glory of God.

Anyone floating upon that vast body of light – anyone, that is, with wings powerful enough to propel them to that nearly impossible height where the Ocean of Light exists -- could detect a current in the light as it swirls and twists about. So wide is the ocean that following its current means traveling across thousands of miles, riding immense, radiant waves which crash and sparkle as they urge the light onward.

At the ocean's far edge a deep, massive roar announces a spectacular finale for the river. There the light spills out and back down toward Heaven's surface. Falling from its immense height, a Niagara of pure energy that seems to go on forever, the River of Light again adds brightness, until the mists far below cause everyone to look away, so intensely blazes the divine power.

It is said that somewhere, deep within those Mists of Light, exists the Throne of God.

Close to the waterfall of light, high above the mists, a ledge protruded from a cavern. There, a number of angels congregated around what they called *The Place of First Awareness.*

"Do you think He will create another?" Stondrin asked no one in particular, his bushy eyebrows rising so high they resembled question marks. But then, Stondrin's face wore a perpetual look of curiosity. The other angels sometimes kidded him about his habit of asking about anything and everything, but this time he voiced the question they all pondered.

Several of them shook their heads. God's actions of late both puzzled and excited them.

"I believe that's why I'm here," one of the angels replied. "I received a summons from Michael not long ago to come as soon as possible."

"That's a major speech for you, Rendall," Stondrin teased his friend. The angel ducked his head in embarrassment. "This could be exciting." Rendall spoke little when in a group – unless a question had been asked him -- but everyone knew he had the gifts of wisdom and teaching.

One of the newer angels approached Stondrin. "Why is it so important to have Rendall involved?"

"Because it's amazing what he knows," Stondrin responded. "Any question about Heaven can be answered by him. For example: How deep is the Ocean of Light? Rendall knows precisely. How far does the River of Light fall in its journey toward the mists? Rendall has measured it himself!"

Stondrin lowered his voice so that only the angel next to him could hear. "He may be shy in public, but when Rendall gets excited about a subject, he can go on and on. Plus, he has a passion for making sure those in his charge learn their lessons well." Stondrin grinned and pointed at the tangle of hair on the teacher's head. "His hair might go everywhere, but he keeps his students on track.

"If Rendall is going to have personal charge of the new angel, God must have something wonderful and grand planned for him." Stondrin raised his voice slightly as he turned toward the Mists. "Who knows, maybe this new addition will move us another step closer to completing the *Age of Preparation.*"

All the angels knew about the *Age of Preparation.* They had learned their creation played a crucial part in this Age. Truth be known, however, it was the only Age any of them had ever been a part of.

"Rendall," the curious angel called out. "You know more about Heaven than anyone. What existed here before our creation?"

The teacher shook his head. "I know a great deal about the Eternal Country. But the details of Heaven before our *becoming* still remain a mystery to me." He raised a finger to make a point, and several angels grinned. Rendall had gone into teaching mode. "Remember, none of us knows when the next Age will begin, or what it will mean for us. Until God reveals another task to us, we'd all better be committed to fulfilling our present purpose."

He paused to make sure he had their attention. "Nothing is more important than worshiping God and staying true to our purpose."

CHAPTER TWO

"Take him!"

Deep underground, in the heart of a cavern filled with light, the attacker appeared as if from nowhere. He reached for the archangel's back and tried to knock him out of the air.

Michael spun in a smooth motion that looked unhurried. He came out of it, wings steadying him automatically. He balanced himself, raised one foot and kicked hard at his attacker. No, he corrected himself with surprise, there were four attackers! They had burst out of the River of Light flowing through the cavern floor, hoping to surprise their prey.

Remarkable reflexes took over, however, and the angel flew straight down toward the other three still left in the fight. The fourth moaned in pain, holding his right knee where the angel's kick had landed with incredible force.

"Watch out!" -- "Get out of my way!" – "Not me. I'm not the target!"

The three attackers had planned for the angel to fly up and away from them. Instead, with his unexpected change of direction, they found themselves confronted by one of the biggest, strongest angels in all of Heaven. A no-nonsense face topped with close-cropped hair darted down toward one of them, then lifted without warning and smashed into a jaw. At the same time, he used his wings to cover the second attacker's eyes while snaking out an arm and grabbing the last would-be warrior. Once in his grasp, nothing and no one could pull free. The hapless victim closed his eyes as the archangel propelled him at the one blinded by wings in his face.

At the last moment, Michael snatched his wings aside and the two attackers-turned-victims collided. They fell to the cavern floor beside their companions, who were crawling toward the River of Light to bathe their wounds.

"Thought you could best me with an ambush, eh?" the big angel growled.

The other four looked at him with varying degrees of admiration. "I didn't think anyone could beat four angels at once," one of them said. "You're still the best."

"One of the best," the short-haired angel corrected. Truth was important. "Only one of the best. I remember when . . . ." He stopped speaking and turned his head to the side as he listened to a Voice meant only for him. When it finished, he turned back to the others and abruptly changed the subject.

"It's time," he said. "Let's go."

The four angels groaned at the words. "Have a heart, Michael," one of them said. "Let us take a few moments to heal in the River of Light."

Their victor smiled at them, but still shook his head. "That's your fault, not mine. You should have thought of the *becoming* before planning this foolish attempt to beat me."

"Didn't you ever do something foolhardy like this?" asked the first angel, still rubbing his knee as the River flowed over it in gentle waves. The swelling had already decreased by half.

"Sure I did . . . but I always won," retorted the big angel. "Now, let's get going."

The voice seemed to float down from high above. "You're not forgetting about me, are you?"

The group looked up to see the long-haired angel descending

from the roof of the cavern. A smile played across his face as he surveyed the scene. "I told the four of you it would be almost impossible to take him by surprise. He's always ready for the unexpected."

"If we don't hurry, we won't be ready for the *becoming*," the short-hair angel retorted. "I repeat, let's go!"

Five of the angels rose as one toward the cavern's exit high above them. The last of them, however, remained on the floor of the cavern, nursing his wounds. A slender angel with deep-set eyes, he always looked intense. "One day, Michael," he said in a voice made more menacing by its softness. "Just wait . . . one day."

"Shi'intor, up here with the rest of us." The angel looked up to see his captain motioning for him to follow. Now was not the time, he thought. Plastering a smile on his face, Shi'intor obeyed.

———

Darkness comes from . . . nowhere. It seeps into . . . nowhere. But it now exists for the first time as a . . . possibility. It waits . . . .

———

Had a person from Earth been able to see them, the angels in *The Place of First Awareness* would have seemed gloriously beautiful. Swift and strong, they carried out God's commands with a divine perfection that only complemented the light pulsing around and through them.

From the angels' point of view, however, differences in size and function could be clearly seen. One or two -- Michael, the archangel, for example -- towered above even the strongest. Rumor had it that he, too, might be interested in this *becoming*.

Stondrin looked around for the archangel as he and the other angels began backing away from the center of the ancient, divinely-drawn circle. They could feel the power building and concentrating. "If Michael wants to see this, he'd better hurry," he muttered.

As the words left his mouth, someone else shouted, "Here he comes!"

Excited whispers ran through the group. Light streamed from the interior of the cavern. Michael approached the angels, each stride covering huge amounts of ground. Muscles rippled with every swing of an arm. Power fit him like a well-designed suit of clothes. Closely cropped hair might frame a face with an intense, no-nonsense look. But the smile which broke out on occasion showed the love he had for his angelic charges.

All eyes, however, turned not to him, but to the figure keeping pace with him. As powerful as Michael, taller by a head, light flowed from this being as he walked. Long strands of golden hair whipped through the air behind him. His eyes constantly swiveled, taking in everything and missing nothing. Wherever he went, angels approached, asking for instructions and basking in his power. His beauty only became greater as he nodded to those under his command, and they responded by roaring out his name.

"Lucifer! Among angels, your power is unmatched. We praise our God who made you. Lucifer! Lucifer!"

Lucifer smiled and acknowledged their praise.

CHAPTER THREE

"Michael and I are here to watch the next *becoming*."

Lucifer looked at his friend as he said this. Everyone knew the two sometimes seemed to act as one, so alike were they. Created on the same day, God had instilled in them immense power and beauty. Their ability to lead instilled passion in their followers. The love they had for those under their commands forged strong bonds of loyalty. Lucifer's extra strength, power and beauty mattered not to Michael – or to any other of the angels. For at that time, selfish pride had no place among Heaven's citizens.

"It is time!" Michael announced. He and Lucifer led the others in kneeling around the center of the *Place of First Becoming*. As he joined the circle, Stondrin knew each of them, like himself, thought only of that special moment when they *became*.

"Look at the power," Lucifer whispered. "I never get tired of looking at the power!"

The others drew back a little as the power on the ledge coalesced into an incandescent ball of light. The glorious music of *becoming* accompanied the light, swelling until it filled all of Heaven. . Then . . . .

First awareness.

Light. Everywhere.

Light beginning to focus.

Who am I? What is my place here . . . in Heaven?

Something . . . someone in front of me. Oh! They are beautiful! Are these . . . angels? Is that the word for them?

They look so perfect. Golden hair. Dark flecks of gold in their eyes. And their pupils! They shine with the purest gleam of silver, like windows of the soul.

But – somehow – they look different from me.

With the dimming of the light, the watchers gasped. The most unusual angel Heaven had ever seen fluttered a few feet above the ledge.

"Grab him, Stondrin!" Lucifer ordered. Thin, spindly, the newest angel looked to be in danger of being blown off the ledge by the light gusting around him. "Be careful, though. Don't hurt him."

Lucifer needn't have worried. Oblivious to everyone else, the angel stared in rapture at the mists below the ledge. At his *becoming*, every angel did the same. For in those mists each new creation could see and hear God. Others only heard a loud roar; they could see nothing but swirling, cascading light. In that first encounter with God, the angel would receive both his name and the purpose for which he had been created.

Every inhabitant of heaven had a purpose given them by God. They might be required to do other tasks, as well. But all knew their purpose overrode everything else they might accomplish. In some cases, the purpose of an angel might be known to all. In certain other instances, however, an angel could be commanded by God to keep private why he had been created and what his ultimate reason for existence might be. No one questioned divinely-given responsibility. All delighted in living out their love of God by always being ready to use that purpose to glorify their Heavenly Father. And, each angel had been assured there would come a time when they would fulfill their reason for being created.

After a long moment, the new angel turned to face the assembled group. "My name is Grisson," he stated.

"Hail, Grisson," the angels responded in the timeless ritual. "We praise our God who brought you into being."

"What is God's purpose for you?" asked Lucifer.

"I . . ." a momentary hitch stole into Grisson's voice. "I don't know yet."

Stunned silence followed this pronouncement.

"What in Heaven's name are you talking about?" Stondrin asked. A firm hand fell hard on his shoulder, cutting off whatever else he'd intended to say. Stondrin looked up to see Michael put a warning finger to his lips.

"I think the new angel's listening to another Voice," the archangel whispered.

A moment later, Grisson whirled around to face the others once again. "God has called me to His throne," he announced. And with that, he unfurled his wings and exploded off the ledge.

Even Lucifer could not follow the angel's flight. One moment Grisson stood before them, a thin, weak-looking angel. The next moment, the onlookers could only see a dwindling speck disappearing into the mists.

"I have never seen speed like that from any creature of Heaven," Stondrin said in awe.

"Nor I," admitted Michael.

Lucifer motioned to the others to gather around him. "Were any of you called into God's presence the moment you came into being?" A shake of the head came from everyone in the group.

"Have any of you ever seen such an angel before?" Again a chorus of "no" answered him.

"This unusual *becoming*, plus the thousands of angels God has created lately, makes me believe my purpose for being will soon be fulfilled.

"At last," Lucifer breathed, "I can serve my God in the way I've always wanted."

For a moment, quiet reigned on the ledge.

Then, a barely audible voice said, "I'd give almost anything to be able to fly like that."

Stondrin turned to see Volthra'an, a wistful look on his face, gazing at the spot Grisson had occupied a moment before. He knew the tall, thin angel to be an acknowledged master of organization. Volthra'an always ensured that Michael's orders were carried out by the other angels. His flying, however, left something to be desired. Volthra'an could be seen practicing maneuvers long after others had left the practice field in the cavern. But the extra time put in never seemed to make a difference.

"Be careful what you wish for, friend," Stondrin said. "Instead, thank God for your own unique ability."

Neither angel noticed Lucifer listening to the exchange.

———

Darkness deeper than the blackest night. Nothing existing in a place yet to be created. And yet, the sound begins. Harsh, grinding, moaning . . . seeking. At home in the blackness. But now . . . intensely hungry. Waiting for the summons it hopes will come.

———

Grisson leaped off the ledge. His Father had summoned him. Where most angels would have glided down toward the mists, the newest angel maneuvered his wings so quickly they seemed to blur into one. Following the divine call, he twisted and darted through light so bright he could no longer see, trusting in his Creator to bring him safely before the throne.

As he flew, his mind kept pace. *Why did the other angels look at me as if I were different? Am I supposed to have a purpose? What does God want with me?*

The questions kept rolling through his mind until suddenly, without warning, the mists parted and Grisson found himself in the vast throne room of God. The River of Light had disappeared, no longer needed. God's Presence illuminated everything in Grisson's vision. Wherever the angel looked, God *was*. At the extreme height of his vision, God observed him. Looking as far as possible to the left and the right, God beckoned to him. The angel skidded to a halt, overwhelmed and humbled, fearful and exultant. The incredible majesty of God drove the angel to his knees. "Holy," he proclaimed. "Almighty God, You are holy and worthy to be praised."

His words were echoed again and again by the huge, wondrous creatures surrounding the throne. Seraphim with six wings floated everywhere. Two of the wings covered their feet; two others covered their face, preventing Grisson from seeing their features; the last two wings moved constantly as they flew in an intricate formation around God's Throne.

Grisson bowed his head once again in worship, even as he continued to look at his Creator and the Lord's ineffable majesty. And then God spoke . . . .

———

The little angel looked around him. He stood in a chamber made completely of rock. Perhaps it had been carved out of the side of a mountain. A gurgling could be heard in the walls, and a drop of liquid light oozed from the ceiling. Grisson assumed the River of Light flowed somewhere close by. In truth, however, he had no idea where he was, nor could he remember how he'd gotten there. To come to think of it, he wasn't even sure how long he had knelt before God's throne, worshipping and thirstily drinking in God's love. He felt rejuvenated by the experience, ready to do something for God. But how could he? The room contained no entrance or exit. He was trapped and alone.

"How are you feeling?"

Grisson's head whipped around. Before him stood an angel he'd never seen before. He didn't think he would ever get used to these sudden changes! "I actually feel great; ready to work for God," he replied.

The angel before him glowed with power . . . and something else. Grisson couldn't pin down exactly what it was. But in some way, his visitor looked different from all the other angels he had seen during his brief time in Heaven.

"My name is LeSage," the angel announced. Though he faced Grisson, his eyes seemed to be looking off into the distance, as if he saw and listened to someone else. "One of my purposes is sometimes to speak for God to the other angels."

Grisson noticed that LeSage nodded his head from time to time, as if to verify he had understood the Voice only he could hear. After several moments, the angel's eyes turned and focused on Grisson.

"Think of this conversation as a way to help you assimilate what you heard and saw in God's throne room," LeSage said. "After we've finished your debriefing, God will transport us back to the *Place of First Becoming*."

Grisson nodded, though he still felt confused. "Where, exactly, are we?" he asked.

"Somewhere in the Eternal Country. And honestly, that's all I know," LeSage admitted, smiling a bit. "The main thing to keep in mind at all times is that God knows *exactly* where we are, so we never have to worry." He pointed behind Grisson . "Go ahead and sit down. We'd might as well be comfortable while we talk."

Grisson turned around and tried hard not to jump in surprise. Two chairs waited for LeSage and him. He sat down in the nearest one. "Okay," he sighed, "what should we talk about?"

"Let's begin with what you took away from your first experience with God."

The little angel paused for a long moment, trying to gather his thoughts. Then he said, "I remember God's love filling me completely." His silver eyes glistened with tears as the memory swept over him. "I remember thinking, This is where I belong. I wish I could stay here forever, worshipping my Lord, my God."

LeSage nodded. "Very good. God wants you to remember, above anything else, that He loves you." He moved his chair closer and leaned forward. "Grisson, God's love for you will never change. No matter what happens, no matter what the circumstances, God's love for you will *never* change."

By this time, the angel's eyes were only inches from Grisson's face. The little angel swallowed hard. Then he nodded. "I will always remember."

LeSage continued to stare intently at Grisson. "I think you mean that," he said finally. "And that's good, because your very survival depends on it."

The angel definitely had Grisson's attention now! But instead of continuing to talk about the little angel's survival, LeSage settled back in his chair and casually asked, "Now, do you have any other questions while we're still here?"

The sudden change in subject actually helped Grisson. It brought him up short and forced him to go over once again everything that had happened since his Becoming. One thought among all the others kept rising to the top. It hammered at him, demanding to be expressed. The question embarrassed him, but he had to get an answer now, while no one else could hear their conversation. Gathering his courage, Grisson finally blurted, "What is my purpose? You say that you speak for God sometimes. So, why have I been created?"

The answer, when it came, froze him in shock.

"I'm not sure why, but you are the only angel God has ever created who does not have a purpose. Whether or not you ever have one is in your hands."

Hope began to blossom in Grisson. "So you're saying one day God may give me . . . ."

LeSage stood and put out his hand, halting Grisson's question. "In the time to come, Grisson, you will face hard choices. But remember God's love. If you can trust in Him always, one day your reason for being will become evident to all."

"I will trust in Him," Grisson whispered with as much assurance as he could muster. "And I will always love Him."

The walls of the cavern room began to thin, and a moment later, the mists grew bright once more around Grisson. He heard the roar of the light as it fell near the *Place of First Becoming*. Then, dimly, LeSage's voice whispering to him, "Grisson, your purpose will be decided by you. You may share that you do not have a purpose with close friends, but tell no one of the entire conversation. And remember God's love . . . remember God's love . . ."

CHAPTER FOUR

Grisson found himself back on the ledge, surrounded by other angels. Most of them jumped, startled to find him in their midst. Lucifer only nodded at him and smiled, his long hair wreathed in a golden glow.

"Conversation with God?" he asked. Grisson nodded.

"Supposed to keep it to yourself?" he added. The spindly angel nodded again, venturing a smile in return.

Lucifer said, "Don't worry. I've had a few of those conversations myself. So has Michael."

The archangel put a friendly hand on Grisson's shoulder. "Lucifer's right. Don't worry about it. We understand."

"Well, *we* don't!" Any assurance Grisson had begun to feel went up in smoke. He turned to see Stondrin marching up to him, his eyebrows raised to full height. "As far as we know, out of all the hundreds of thousands of angels ever created, you three are the only ones to have a private conversation with God. The rest of us want to know what took place at God's throne."

Stondrin eased up close beside him and whispered, "Come on, you can tell us. After all, we're your friends. We were here for your *becoming*."

"All right, Stondrin, that's enough!" Michael barked. "One day your curiosity is going to get you in big trouble."

Stondrin sighed good humouredly. "Okay, chief. I'll back off."

"Rendall," Michael continued. "It's time to begin Grisson's lessons. I want them completed by the time the River of Light has made one cycle."

Grisson glanced at the angel Michael addressed. The first thing he noticed was the hair. It looked as if no two strands went in the same direction. What kind of angel would have hair like that? When he lowered his gaze to the face, however, he saw his future teacher looking back steadily, as if trying to appraise his new pupil. Grisson dropped his eyes, embarrassed to be caught staring.

"Why so soon, Michael?" As usual, Stondrin asked the question everyone else wanted to ask. "Most of us had thirty or forty light cycles to learn about Heaven."

"You can blame that on me," Lucifer said. "For some reason, God wants Grisson ready as soon as possible."

He raised his voice, until everyone in that region of the Eternal Country could hear God's most powerful angel. "Those of you who serve under me, know this," he thundered. "I have reason to believe *The Age of Preparation* will soon be over. More than ever, be diligent in fulfilling your purpose!"

Grisson watched in wonder as the most magnificent creation in all of Heaven shouted instructions. Lucifer's beauty, strength and leadership fascinated him. Even among other creatures of radiance, Lucifer outshone them all.

"Come on." A no-nonsense voice brought Grisson out of his trance. Rendall motioned for him to follow. "We've got a lot to teach you in only a short while." He headed into the cavern. "If you're as quick at learning as you are at flying, you'll have no trouble."

Grisson sighed and turned to follow. Things were certainly moving at a fast pace.

The angels watched as Grisson and Rendall disappeared into the cavern. All were wondering at the strange turn of events.

"That is the last angel God will ever create."

Heads snapped around in astonishment. Michael grabbed the speaker by his shoulder. "Explain yourself, LeSage," he demanded.

LeSage calmly regarded the big archangel with the same stoic demeanor he always displayed. "Michael, you've heard me make these kinds of pronouncements before. For whatever reason, God tells me these things. And when He does, it's my purpose to share them with all of you." His solemn face took in both Michael and Lucifer. "In some way I still don't understand, a great change is coming to the Eternal Country . . . and to all of us."

"What's he talking about?" "When will this take place?" Excited voices filled the ledge, everyone speaking at once.

Michael motioned for quiet. He waited a moment, took a deep breath to respond . . . and stopped when a hand squeezed his arm hard.

"Listen," Lucifer whispered.

The archangel turned toward the mists. Lucifer had done the same thing. From within the gusting beams of light, the two heard a divine summons. They glanced at one another, nodded and, as one, dove off the ledge, angling down and away toward the bright light below.

"I'd give anything to know what's going on," Stondrin said.

"I have a feeling we'll all be knowing before long," LeSage answered, his voice so soft no one but Stondrin could hear.

God's vast Throne Room seemed to stretch to infinity. As large and magnificent as the two angels were, their beauty and power became insignificant in God's Presence. Michael and Lucifer worshiped their Creator as they knelt before Him in love and submission. Above them the Seraphim echoed their praise, until it seemed impossible to tell where one left off and the other began. Heavenly music swelled to match the praise of the

Seraphim. Finally, in the midst of the eternal splendor, God spoke to His two archangels, giving them instructions for the coming light cycles. At the end of the conversation, Michael trembled with joy and anticipation. But when he looked at Lucifer, he noticed the big angel seemed subdued, maybe even troubled.

"Rise, Michael and Lucifer." LeSage appeared before them, motioning with his hands for them to stand up. "In a moment, we'll move to the chamber. But I'm to let you know that my words spoken in that chamber reflect God's will completely."

Both angels nodded as one. As the throne room began to fade from their vision, God's love once again surrounded them. Wrapped in that divine cocoon of the Father, they found themselves transported to the rock cavern with LeSage.

Michael, Lucifer and LeSage settled themselves in the three chairs waiting for them. Both archangels stayed silent. Michael wanted to hear LeSage's words. Lucifer, for his part, continued to look troubled.

"God has decreed that I will not remember this conversation when we leave this cavern," LeSage began. "I tell you this for two reasons. First, given the delicate nature of what we'll be talking about, you don't have to worry about my having what amounts to a very private knowledge about both of you, as well as the future. Second, this serves as a reminder that you must not ask me questions about this later on, as I'll have no idea what you're talking about."

God's messenger turned and faced both angels. "It has been confirmed that what I'd said earlier is true. Grisson is the last angel God will create. The two of you were God's first creations. Hundreds of thousands of angels later, Grisson is the last. The three of you, however, are inexorably linked together for ages to come."

Lucifer ventured a question. "Do you know in what way we will be associated with the little angel?"

LeSage turned his head upward, listening to the Voice only

he could hear. Then he nodded and said, "All I can tell you is this: how you are associated with Grisson depends upon the three of you. Very soon, you each will have a decision to make; that is why God has brought you here." LeSage's voice swelled with passion. "God tells you, above all, to remember His love always."

As the words were spoken, even though they were in the chamber and not in God's throne room, both Michael and Lucifer felt an overwhelming wave of love engulf them. Shaking and exultant, God's first two creations responded. "God, we will always love you and serve you."

"Lucifer, what is your purpose?" A sudden change of subject by LeSage.

Startled, Lucifer hesitated a moment, then responded, "My purpose is to rule for God one day."

"I know your memory is better than that." The words, spoken gently, still had their intended purpose. Lucifer dropped his head in embarrassment.

"God said my purpose is to serve Him by guiding and watching over a new creation."

"Lucifer, raise your head and look at me." Lucifer obeyed, wondering why LeSage was speaking to him in this way. "This may be the most important conversation you and I will ever have. God wants you to hear these words and understand them well."

LeSage's eyes went out of focus, as if he saw Another. "God's purpose for you gives you great responsibility and reward. The purpose as *you* stated it leads to your destruction forever. God does not wish for any being in His creation to undergo that fate."

Lucifer seemed puzzled. "I . . . I don't understand the difference," he stammered.

"You have been created to serve God, Lucifer," LeSage explained. "In guiding and watching over His new creation, you will fulfill your purpose and glorify God. But it is to be done as service for others, not rule for yourself." Once again, God's Love surrounded the two angels.

"We do not deserve your love, " Michael blurted out. "God, I know you can hear us. We can never hope to repay You for the life You've given us."

"Michael, Lucifer." Though they looked into the eyes of LeSage, both angels felt Eternity looking back through them. Those eyes bored into them. "A new Age is about to begin. Remember God's love."

Lucifer bowed his head. "I will serve the Lord."

CHAPTER FIVE

As they made their way deeper into the cavern, it puzzled Grisson to see the light growing in intensity. "How can this be?" he asked Rendall.

The angel raised his hand and pointed at some rocks jutting out from the side of the cavern wall. He gestured for Grisson to move in that direction.

"Good question. It will be the basis of your first – and most important – lesson." He moved to one of the rocks and sat, motioning for his pupil to do the same. "In a moment, you'll see many angels attempting a number of different tests. I don't want you to be distracted, so we'll stay here for the time being."

Rendall leaned forward on the rock. "Always remember this," he said solemnly. "The River of Light is everywhere throughout Heaven. There is no place or individual that is not touched or influenced by the River." He gestured toward the walls of the cavern. "Even here, deep underground, the River makes itself seen and felt. And it is like this wherever you choose to go in the Eternal Country. Do you understand?"

Grisson nodded. "But why is this such an important lesson?"

"AHA!" Rendall's shout so startled Grisson that he fell off the rocky outcrop he'd been sitting on.

"What's the matter with you?" Grisson asked. As he scrambled to regain his seat, Grisson wondered if his teacher could really be as smart as others said.

"By your response, you tell me you don't understand!" Rendall continued. He seemed unaware of the effect his outburst had on the new angel.

"Maybe this will help. God has made the River of Light for us as a reminder of His purpose. No matter where we are, high or low, close to the mists or far away, the River is there. And that means God's purpose is being carried out."

Grisson's eyes widened. Now he understood. "In other words, there is nowhere you can ever go in Heaven, where God's purpose is not at work." ."

Rendall nodded to himself. The lesson had been learned.

"God is here, Grisson. As the light flows all around us, so does God's presence and purpose. We can't see Him, but He always sees us. Every time you look at the River of Light, remember this lesson."

He moved his face to within inches of his pupil. "*Remember this lesson*, Grisson. I don't have a lot of time to spend with you, reinforcing principle after principle. For whatever reason, God has decreed that you must quickly learn as much as possible."

"I'll remember," Grisson promised. "The River reminds us that God's purpose is constant, even when we don't understand it."

Grisson hopped off his seat and ran to catch up with Rendall. Satisfied that his ward had learned the first lesson, Rendall had wasted not a moment. Instead, he hurried off, turned a corner and disappeared. Grisson, rushing to make up the distance between them, turned the same corner – and fell off the ledge.

"What–?" A sheer drop of horrendous proportions stretched out beneath his feet. He had but a moment to react. But the newest angel in Heaven blurred his wings and instinctively took a step back. To Rendall, it looked as if Grisson had stepped onto the air for a moment, then returned to the ledge.

"You're faster than any I've seen yet." He grinned at Grisson's still startled expression. "Don't worry, that particular corner's a little joke we play on all the new angels."

The two glanced down at the plain far below. "I remember when I rounded that corner for the first time and felt nothing but empty space beneath me. It surprised me so much that I fell halfway before being able to get my wings to work." He patted Grisson on the shoulder. "Don't worry; you'll do just fine."

"Now," Rendall said, turning serious once again, "tell me what you see."

Grisson hardly knew where to begin. Below him stretched a great plain. As far as the eye could see, angels flew, marched and jogged in formation. Above him, the River of Light entered the cavern from an unseen opening and wound its way down the steep, rocky sides until it finally reached the floor. There, the River seemed bent on interrupting the angels in their maneuvers.

He watched as the liquid light, twisting this way and that, ever changing its course, surprised one of the angels. It suddenly ran beneath him. Deprived of solid ground, the angel tottered for a moment, then fell into the River. The angel's companions roared with laughter. They dunked the hapless victim several times as he tried to escape. Finally, he drifted far enough away from his friends to be able to climb back onto the cavern floor. Instead of being upset, however, Grisson noticed that the angel had risen from the cavern floor with a joyous expression on his face. His whole body glowed as light streamed from him and back into the River.

"All right. That's enough loafing. Back to work!" Over all this scene of mass confusion flew a stocky, powerful angel. Bellowing orders, pushing or pulling angels as he showed them how to avoid falling into the River, the angel's eyes seemed to take in everything at once.

"What do you see?" Rendall repeated quietly.

Grisson thought before answering. Rendall's question, he

knew, was not an idle one. The teacher had but a short time to complete his training. So every question would be important, designed to reinforce the learning process.

Grisson's eyes took in the scene once more. Then he understood. Pointing to the River of Light, he said, "I see the presence of God throughout this cavern, overseeing everything that's done."

Rendall heaved a huge sigh. "Well . . . you are, indeed, a fast learner. Now, let's drop in on Stavros and his troops." Stepping off the ledge, he dropped straight down, unfurling his wings at the last instant so that he floated gently to the cavern floor. It startled Rendall to see Grisson emulating his every move -- and looking as if he'd done it for thousands of light cycles. "Who's the new angel?" A voice that sounded as if the user were gargling with gravel cut through all the noise.

"Stavros, this is Grisson, God's latest creation." Rendall turned to the spindly angel and explained, "This is Stavros. He is in charge of training all the angels how to maneuver better with their wings. He's also Lucifer's second-in-command."

Stavros acted as if he hadn't heard a single word Rendall said. Instead, he barked, "Okay, Grisson, see that line over there? Get in it and follow what the other angels are doing."

Where the River of Light pooled slightly, angels were flying hundreds of feet straight up. Once above the pool, they turned over on their backs, folded their wings and plummeted toward the glistening light. At a height of about twenty feet, the angels would try to pull out of their dive. Some made it; even more, however, couldn't stop their free fall and, with a deafening splash, careened into the River of Light. When that happened, the angels would climb out of the pool, go back to the end of the line, and patiently wait their turn again.

"Watch them carefully," Stavros instructed. "See what mistakes they make. When you think you're brave enough to try it, and sure enough to succeed, let me know. Until then, don't bother me. I'm busy."

Stavros started to walk away when he heard Grisson say, "In that case, I'm ready to try it now."

Stavros turned in astonishment and the thin, spindly angel took a quick step back. "Angel, don't waste my time," he thundered. You don't even know what you're talking about."

"I'd really appreciate it if you'd give him a chance." This voice came from a different direction. "I think he just may be right." More astonishment! Rendall supported this new angel in his preposterous bluff!

Stavros shook his head. "I don't know what's going on here, but we've never done anything like this before. And you, Rendall," Stavros stopped to glower at the teacher. "I can't believe you'd set his training back by letting Grisson begin with a painful failure."

"I'm not setting his training back." Rendall refused to back down before the flying instructor.

Stavros spread his arms to encompass all the angels in the cavern. "Grisson, these angels have been practicing here for a long time. Most take at least ten light cycles just to perfect flying, diving and stopping quickly." His eyes flicked toward Volthra'an for an instant. "Others take much longer.

"Then there are the five or six light cycles dedicated to formations ." Stavros started to pace. Rendall groaned inwardly. They were in for a long speech if he didn't do something quickly. "And then probably another twenty light cycles just to . . . ."

"Lucifer has commanded that I complete all his training in one light cycle." The words came quietly, but Rendall could see they had their intended effect. Stavros groaned, shut his eyes for a moment, then nodded.

"Everybody, quiet!" he roared. The whole cavern became silent as the angels turned their attention to their leader. "This is Grisson." Stavros pointed to the little angel. "He has just been created. And he is going to attempt the free-fall test -- without ever having practiced it."

Laughter erupted at Stavros' words. Grisson could feel a flush slowly cover his face.

"Don't worry." Rendall came up behind Grisson and laid a gentle hand on his shoulder. "I wouldn't let you do this if I thought you'd fail. God has already given you some special qualities. That's why He knows you don't need much time in training." He patted Grisson on the back. "Do your best."

Grisson nodded, then began winging his way toward the pool. "Hey, is your nickname Crashmaster?" someone called out. He tried to ignore the jibe, but felt his face turning red once more. Reflecting on it later, Grisson admitted embarrassment caused him to do what he did next. When he reached the pool, he turned and flew straight up, not stopping at the hundred-foot mark.

"Hey!" he could hear Stavros shouting at him. "You don't need to go so high." Grisson ignored him and continued upward, finally passing the ledge. Even at that lofty height he didn't stop, but continued to climb until his wings brushed the top of the cavern's roof.

Far below, he could see the upturned faces of the angels. Many of them closest to the pool moved away as quickly as possible, including Stavros. They all saw nothing but a crazy newcomer.

No, not all. With his angelic vision, he recognized Rendall still standing next to the pool. Quietly confident of Grisson's ability.

He needed more than his teacher's confidence, however, if he was going to succeed. "Father, I know you are here," Grisson whispered. "I trust in You to help me." Then he folded his wings and leaned backwards.

Grisson could feel himself begin to plummet toward the pool thousands of feet below.

Stavros watched in horror as the little angel streaked toward the ground. "He'll never make it," he rasped to Rendall. "At that height, he'll need to start pulling out at about 100 feet. And at the speed he's traveling, it's too difficult to judge distance." He looked at the other angels around the pool. "Move back farther. This one is going to set the all-time splash record."

Still, Rendall stood by the pool.

All watched as Grisson continued to fall. He hurtled toward the cavern floor, his descent becoming ever faster. At the five-hundred-foot mark, he seemed as still as if he were gliding above the River of Light, his wings tight against his body. At the two-hundred-foot mark, Rendall heard Stavros whisper, "Now, little angel. Now."

But Grisson made no move to stop his fall.

A deadly quiet pervaded the cavern. All watched the body of the angel streak toward the pool. One-hundred feet; fifty feet; ten feet passed. At the last moment, with a huge "SNAP," Grisson twisted his body impossibly erect, unfolded his wings and came to a complete stop. As he floated just inches above the pool, shouts of admiration and cries of surprise from the watching angels filled the cavern.

Then a second surprise. Stavros smiled! No one had ever seen such a thing!

"Come over here, Mister Flyer." Motioning to him, the huge angel actually laughed and clapped Grisson on the back. The force of the friendly blow nearly knocked him to the ground, but Stavros didn't notice. Instead, he was saying, "You have to show me how you did that. Never have I seen such a performance! Never!"

Rendall forced his way between the two angels. Stavros' enthusiasm threatened to flatten Grisson if something weren't done. "Stavros," he shouted. "Remember Lucifer's order. I haven't got much time to finish his training." He began dragging the bewildered Grisson away from the pool before anyone could protest.

"Grisson," he instructed. "See the ledge above you?" Grisson nodded. "Fly to it as fast as possible and wait for me there."

Stavros started to protest, but Grisson no longer stood

before them. In the time it took for him to raise his head and follow Grisson's flight, the little angel had already reached the ledge and now awaited further instructions.

"Rendall," Stavros said in reproach, "you know there's more than just flying and formations that go on in the cavern. What about the rest of his training?"

The teacher grimaced. "Don't worry, I'll test him in that area, too. If he flunks it, we'll be back." He shook his head. "That's one test I'm not looking forward to administering. I have a feeling he'll pass it, pardon the pun, with flying colors."

"I don't know what's going on," the burly angel again muttered to Rendall. "But I'm not sure I like it!"

Rendall nodded in agreement. "I don't know what's happening either. I'm just assigned to be his teacher. But he learns fast and seems to have great insight into what is most important." Rendall then unfurled his wings and began to fly toward the ledge. Looking back, he said, "Thanks for the help, Stavros."

"I didn't help him at all," Stavros protested.

"Not him. Thanks for helping me." The words floated down to the huge angel and his troops.

A tall, thin angel stood to the side, taking in everything. "It's not fair. It's just not fair," Volthra'an said to no one in particular. Then he turned away and began what he knew could only end up being another futile attempt to learn to fly faster and better.

Dalsa'in winged his way over the River of Light. He sometimes followed the river on its course through the Eternal Country simply for the joy of seeing, once again, the stunning vistas of Heaven. *So, a new Age may be coming soon. I wonder what changes it holds for me?* he mused. As he thought further on the subject, a deep contentment filled Dalsa'in. Then he chuckled softly to himself. "Content" was his usual state.

He remembered the moment Lucifer had picked him to be one of his captains. Other angels had been surprised at Lucifer's choice, but not as surprised as Dalsa'in, himself. Truth be told, Dalsa'in loved being a part of the crowd, not standing out from it. He did his job faithfully, one light-cycle followed another, and contentment filled him completely. Not a bad existence.

The task of captain had, at first, overwhelmed him. But as he worked with the leaders under him and saw how efficient their groups became under his guidance, Dalsa'in finally understood the wisdom in Lucifer's choosing him for an expanded role in the angels' continued training. The result for him: contentment! He chuckled once more.

A sound just behind him caused the angel to turn. A column of brilliant, glistening particles began rising from The River of Light. Dalsa'in floated before this new marvel, trying to decide what meaning or purpose it held. He did not have to wonder long. The surface of the column grew brighter, the gold and silver of its hues became richer, more pronounced. Deep within the column, images swam together forming . . . . With a shock, Dalsa'in realized he was looking through a divine window into the center of Heaven. He saw a Throne, and One who sat upon it. Contentment blossomed into adoration as the angel gazed upon the majesty of God almighty.

The angel bowed, completely submerged in God's presence. Love, joy, peace, fulfillment – so great were the emotions that washed over and around him, Dalsa'in could not speak. Little by little, the intensity eased, until after a time the angel was able to gasp out, "I love you, Father." As he raised his head, Dalsa'in realized with astonishment no other angels could be seen in the throne room, except God's spokesman, LeSage.

"These words are for you, alone, Dalsa'in, among all the angels," declared LeSage. "After this meeting is over, I will retain no memory of the conversation. Only you and God will know what was spoken here."

Dalsa'in struggled to speak through his astonishment. "I am but an ordinary angel. What have I done to deserve this?"

"God has both a warning and a promise for you. First the warning: God wants you to know, Dalsa'in, your greatest strength has the potential to be your greatest weakness."

Confusion replaced the angel's astonishment. "Would you permit me to ask what that means?," he said.

LeSage's face grew serious. "What would you do if your faithfulness to God no longer brought you contentment?"

"But," Dalsa'in stammered, "that would never happen!"

"You have not answered my question, Dalsa'in."

Shame filled the angel. "I'm sorry. I . . . I've just never thought of that possibility before." He paused a moment, reflecting carefully. Then, his voice firm, he stated, "I love my God, and I want to serve Him. I hope my faithfulness to Him will always come before anything and anyone else in my life – even if it means losing my contentment."

As he said the last words, Dalsa'in felt God's love wash over him once more.

LeSage smiled as he said, "Well said, faithful servant of God. Now here is the promise: if you are, indeed, faithful through everything, you will know more contentment for all of eternity than you have ever before known."

LeSage's voice began fading away, as did his image. But Dalsa'in could hear him say one more thing faintly. "In the Age to come, remember your declaration – and always remember God's love."

The vision of the throne room disappeared. What had been a divine window now turned opaque as The River of Light began to claim the column of sparkling particles once more. And as the river resumed its journey through the Eternal Country, Dalsa'in found himself continuing his meditative flight. Now, however, he definitely had something else to think about!

———

Grisson wanted nothing more than to lie down on the rocky outcropping and close his eyes. He knew, however, the angels assembled far below now watched his every move. He wanted to please Rendall, so he stood as casually as possible, trying to look unaffected by everything that had just transpired.

"Let's back up a bit and get out of eyesight of everyone."

Rendall's words, like the teacher, himself, came floating toward Grisson. He watched Rendall gracefully alight on the ledge. The angel put a wing around Heaven's newest creation and guided him around the corner where they could be unobserved. Once there, he gently pushed Grisson toward the floor. Both teacher and pupil collapsed on the ground, exhausted.

Grisson took several long breaths, then looked sideways at his teacher. "Why so tired, Rendall?" he asked. "After all, I was the one doing all the exercising!" He smiled to take any sting there might have been out of the words.

He needn't have worried. Rendall allowed a small grin to cross his face and shook his head, sending hair flying in every direction. "I may be even more exhausted than you are, Grisson!" he said. "After all, you were pretty sure you knew what you could do. I, on the other hand, had to simply stand and watch you. I couldn't help you, didn't know for sure if you were capable of that flying feat you pulled off, and knew Stavros would have had my hide if you'd failed." He shuddered. "Emotionally, I worked far harder than you did!"

Grisson nodded, then his expression changed. "Rendall, I don't understand something – well, actually there are a great many things I don't understand," he amended. "But this one has puzzled me ever since I saw the angels practicing in the cavern." He paused. "Do you have time to answer this, or should I wait until after training?"

"Go ahead," Rendall said. "I think I know what you're going to ask. If I'm right, the answer to your question will actually be a part of your training." He nodded at the young angel to continue.

"Okay," Grisson said. "I see hundreds of thousands of angels. They are constantly training to better themselves in flying, in fighting and in how to operate in small groups as efficiently as possible." He looked at his teacher. "Am I right?"

Rendall nodded once more. "Your perceptions are correct."

"So," Grisson continued. "My question is: why?"

"Why what?" Rendall asked with a smile, as if he already knew the answer.

Grisson foundered for a moment, unsure of what to say first. "Well, there are actually several 'whys'. Why does God need so many angels? There doesn't seem to be a need for all of us – or, any of us, for that matter. And, why are we practicing fighting? Who is our enemy? After all, we all get along surrounded by God's love. For that matter, why the emphasis on groups, leaders, ranks, captains, and generals? I can't figure out the purpose of all this emphasis on organization." He paused to catch his breath. "Whew! Sorry to lay all that on you, Rendall."

"Don't be sorry. Everything you've asked needs to be explained anyway." Rendall ran fingers through his hair as he thought how to best respond. The hair remained unaffected by the smoothing gesture. It was as if it had a mind of its own.

"First, understand this," Rendall began. "God always has a purpose for everything He does. Over countless light cycles, He has been creating angels and having them undergo rigorous training. Hold on," he said, raising his hand and stopping Grisson from asking another question. "I think I'll answer everything you've asked when I tell you this next fact.

"God has revealed some things to us, but not everything. He says our faith in Him must grow on its own. If we know every piece of the future, faith will not be needed, and we could remain weak in our reliance upon God."

Rendall stood up and raised his index finger. Grisson smiled when he saw the gesture. The angel had gone into teaching mode!

"However," Rendall continued, "God has allowed us to know

that this, the Age of Creation, is but the first of several Ages to come. In one or more of those Ages we may be called upon to fight some enemy, though who could think to try and stand against God and His forces is beyond me." Rendall began to pace back and forth in front of his pupil. "We may be separated from other angels during these battles. Therefore, it's important to be able for each small group to have a leader and for the angels in that group to function smoothly as a unit. Hence, the organization you see."

Grisson raised his hand. Rendall stopped his monologue and raised an eyebrow.

"Yes?"

"Why doesn't God just do all this Himself?" the little angel asked. "After all, He is all-powerful."

"We call that quality of God 'omnipotent,' and I really don't know why God decided to create us and use angels as His servants." He smiled grimly. "Maybe you can ask God that question the next time you see Him."

Grisson paled and blurted out, "Not me! I was just wondering, that's all."

"That's a part of faith," Rendall responded. "I told you, I don't know everything; no one does, not even Lucifer or Michael. Only God is omniscient – all knowing."

CHAPTER SIX

Had anyone been high above the River of Light, where river flowed upward into ocean, they would have seen two things happen almost simultaneously. A flash of angelic white shot over the ocean of light as a huge boat appeared from nowhere, bobbing on the waves. Lucifer and Michael glided down toward the craft, flaring their wings to dramatically decrease their speed.

"Why such a large boat?" Michael wondered aloud. He and Lucifer rarely got the time to fly up to the ultimate gathering place for the River of Light. Each time before, however, the boats provided for them were just large enough to accommodate the tremendous bulk of both angels.

Lucifer shrugged. "I've got more important questions on my mind right now."

The two angels alighted with graceful strength and surveyed the scene. Bathed in a golden hue, the boat reflected the liquid light beneath it. Overhead, the ocean could be seen in mirror image, reflected off a barrier no angel could cross. Around them, light stretched as far as the eye could see. Both heaved a huge sigh at the same time, then laughed when they realized what they'd done.

"Okay," Michael said. "What's on your mind?"

His friend studied him for a moment. "Michael," he finally began, "why do you think God focused so much on correcting the way I described my purpose? I'm still not sure I understand how what I said and what He said are much different."

Michael's face registered shock. "Lucifer, how can you say that?" He rubbed a hand over his face as he thought about how to answer. "God talked about service to Him. You spoke of ruling."

"I don't see much difference in the end, if I'm serving God." Lucifer could certainly be stubborn when he wanted to! "After all, it's just a matter of different ways of looking at it."

The boat spun as the light carrying it surged toward a violent whirlpool. Sparks flew out of the vortex as the speed of the light being drawn into it increased. Heaven's two most powerful angels acted as one, their ability to know what the other would do born from long experience of working with one another. They kicked into the ocean powerfully with their feet and beat the atmosphere with their wings. The result shot the boat far ahead to a calmer part of the ocean.

As if nothing of importance had happened, Lucifer continued. "The main thing for us to remember is that we serve God because He is all-powerful."

Lucifer looked back at the whirlpool of light to see how far they'd come. After a moment, he realized Michael hadn't responded. Lucifer turned back around to say something, and stopped. His closest friend in all of Heaven had a strange expression on his face.

"What?" asked Lucifer.

"That's why you serve God?" Michael said. "Because He's all-powerful?"

Lucifer nodded. "Sure, that's why everyone serves God. He's the most powerful in all the Eternal Country. Because of that, we're supposed to worship Him."

Michael shook his head. "That's not why I serve God at all. I do it because I love Him."

"Well, sure," Lucifer agreed. "That too." And with that, the big angel jumped into the ocean of light, whooping with delight. "Come on, Michael. The light feels great!"

After a moment, Michael followed. But a frown of concern stayed on his face for a good while afterward.

Rendall watched his pupil taking in everything. He nodded his head in silent approval. The little angel had an amazing ability to grasp difficult concepts quickly. *He'd better*, Rendall thought. *He doesn't have the luxury of taking his time assimilating all the different pieces of information coming his way.*

"Could I ask one more question," Grisson said. Then he added, "I promise, this is the last one."

"It's okay," Rendall answered. "And I'm not going to hold you to that last promise. I've seen how your curiosity works. You could be Stondrin, Jr.!"

Grisson flushed. But he asked his question anyway.

"Where does this 'purpose' thing come in for all the angels. And why don't I have one?"

"Let me begin by trying to answer the first part of your question," Rendall said diplomatically, wisely deciding not to point out that his pupil had already broken his promise by asking, not one question, but two. "Remember, God has a purpose in everything He does. His plan is so vast than none of us could ever comprehend all of it. Every angel works with others in his group. But at the same time, God uses each individual angel in ways no other angel is aware of."

Rendall paused, trying to get his words right. "God's plan has many layers. One layer involves us as a group. But other layers are composed of each angel completing his purpose for God's glory. When everyone does his task properly, God's purpose comes to fruition."

Rendall looked his pupil squarely in the eyes. "As for the second part of your question, I have to admit that I have no answer." He saw Grisson's shoulders slump at those words.

"Let me finish, Grisson," he said. "God never does anything

by accident. Your not having a purpose has a purpose." He paused. "Does that make sense to you?"

Grisson slowly nodded. "I think so," he said. "In other words, my not having a purpose can in some way further God's plan, whatever that may be." He looked up once again at his teacher. "Is that right?"

Rendall nodded, relieved. "I *think* that's right."

"One more thing." Grisson rushed his words, embarrassed. "Yes, I know I said the other question would be my last, but everything you talk about brings up something else!"

Rendall grinned but said nothing. Instead he motioned for the new angel to continue.

"You have just stated that everything here in Heaven has a purpose. Is that right?" High up in the cavern, the two angels could hear the sounds of splashing and shouts of encouragement, even though they were out of sight of all the others.

The teacher nodded, wondering where the conversation was headed.

"Okay, if that's true, what is pain's purpose?" Grisson asked. "Why doesn't God take away all pain?"

Rendall looked startled for a moment, then he gathered his thoughts and said, "An excellent question! But let me respond with a question of my own: if there were no pain, how would you know when you made a mistake in flying, landing or fighting?"

"Well, that's easy," Grisson began. "If there were no pain I'd . . . I would . . . ." He shook his head. "I don't know."

His teacher nodded once more. "Exactly. Pain is a teacher. It's not something we love. Sometimes it puts us out of commission for several light cycles as we bathe in the River of Light. But if we pay attention to it, pain will help us not to make the same mistake over and over." Rendall leaned his head against the cavern wall and listened to the River of Light gushing deep within. "God has hinted that there might come a time when there will be no more suffering or pain."

"I'd love that!" Grisson exclaimed.

Rendall put his hand on Grisson's shoulder. "All of us would," he said quietly. "Until that time comes, however, we need to remain faithful to God, in or out of pain."

"I'll try my best," Grisson said quietly. He stood up and squared his shoulders. "And I'll also try to use the pain of my not having a purpose for God's glory!"

"That's the spirit," Rendall said. Then a thought hit him. "Would you like to relax in a different place than here?" he asked.

"It's not that I'm tired now," Grisson explained. "But ever since I "became" there's been no time to stop and . . . and . . . ."

"Think about what you've learned," Rendall finished for him. "If you aren't played out from all the exercise, then I know the perfect place for us to relax; and I can still help you complete most of your training at the same time.

"Follow me," Rendall said, and began winging his way toward the top of the cavern, where the River of Light appeared as if from nowhere. It seemed to Grisson they were getting ready to crash into the roof. But Rendall turned at the last instant and plunged headlong into the Light. Grisson sighed and followed. The surprises were beginning to tire him.

Another surprise awaited him, however, a moment later. He found himself in the middle of a huge plain. Here the River of Light flowed straight up. But that meant . . . surely he had to be wrong . . . Could it really be true that the *Place of First Becoming* and the cavern were now far, far away? He saw his teacher grin and nod in agreement.

"How did we get here so fast?" Grisson wondered aloud.

Rendall pointed upward with one of his wings. "Let's get to our destination first, then I'll explain." He reached out a hand and firmly grabbed one of Grisson's hands. "Few can make this journey easily. I'll add my wing power, but you will have to do most of the work if we are to reach the ocean above us."

Rendall unfolded his wings and instructed Grisson to do the same. The two angels sprang up as one. But before he could even begin to maneuver his wings, Rendall found himself far above the plain. Grisson's wings hummed in the heavenly atmosphere. When Rendall began to add his strength to their flight, both were surprised at the speed they attained. The vast country of Heaven spread out beneath them. The higher they flew, the more beauty they beheld of God's marvelous creation. In the distance, they could see the magnificent Niagara of light, its mists swirling in rainbow splendor. Angels flew everywhere, following the orders of either Michael or Lucifer. Even a cherubim could be seen here and there, flitting about on an errand for God. Soon, the glistening surface of the ocean came into view, and before they knew it, a small boat floated beneath them, seemingly waiting for their presence.

Rendall let go of the little angel's hand and led the way down to the boat. Just enough room existed for the two of them to sit comfortably. The teacher put his back against the mast and dangled his legs over the side. He let the light flow over them as the boat glided across the ocean.

"Is this boat always here, waiting for those who make the journey?" Grisson asked. "And what happens if more than two arrive at the same time? It looks as if things could get a little crowded!" He sat down beside his teacher. The flow of light over his legs and feet seemed to send a constant glow of pleasure throughout his entire being, energizing him.

"We'll sit here for awhile," Rendall said. "Instead of answering your question, let's see if you can figure it out yourself."

Grisson groaned. "Can't you give me an easy answer? Just once?" he pleaded.

"Sorry," Rendall responded, not really sounding sorry at all. "This way, you'll remember what you learn. There is nothing that has happened to you so far that's not been used to teach you something. Everything has a purpose. Everything."

Not everything, Grisson thought. *I don't have a purpose.* But he decided to keep those thoughts to himself. Maybe God would soon be ready to give Grisson a purpose, so that he could be like all the other angels.

"Yes, I know you use everything to teach me about Heaven," said Grisson, regaining his humor. "The way you stepped off that ledge and landed was no accident. Following you showed me how to make that dive from the cavern roof." He grinned at the startled Rendall. "You were setting up both Stavros and me, weren't you?"

"Grisson, shame on you!" Rendall said, turning his face to hide a smile. "I just wanted to help you complete your training in the allotted time." Then he turned serious. "Anyway, back to your question about the boat. Can you remember the most important lesson I've taught you so far?"

The angel answered immediately. "The River of Light reminds us that God is everywhere."

Rendall nodded. "And how does that lesson help us here?"

"That's a little harder," Grisson admitted. He looked around him. Everywhere, light beckoned to him. Their boat climbed a wave, buoyed by shimmering particles. Beneath them, currents sparkled and gleamed as they caressed the vessel. Finally, he said, "God is here. And," he ventured further, "God was with us on our flight here."

"Keep going," his teacher encouraged.

"So, if God knew we were coming here, He would also know we'd need something to rest in."

Then it hit him.

"So," he said with excitement, "God made this boat especially for us!" He looked at Rendall. "That's it, isn't it? That's the lesson I'm supposed to learn."

"Very good, Grisson." Rendall gave an approving nod. "You've learned another important lesson. God always provides for us. He's good enough, and loving enough, to give us even small comforts like this."

Grisson leaned out over the ocean, sighed and let the light

caress his hand. "Then let's take a break and enjoy God's creation."

"We can relax while I teach you one or two more principles. If you pay attention, then we'll lie back and enjoy the rest of the voyage in peace." Rendall motioned for Grisson to sit up.

"First of all," he continued, "'let's get back to the question you asked me down on the plain."

Grisson thought once again about the huge distance they'd covered in only a short time. From the cavern to the Great Plain would normally take half a light cycle. They'd made the journey almost instantaneously. "How is that possible?" he asked.

"It's simple, once you think about it," his teacher said. "All you have to do is realize that everything you see here in Heaven has been created by God – even 'distance'. So if God wants to create a shortcut for us angels, all He has to do is refuse to create 'distance' in one particular place."

Grisson nodded. "Are there any other shortcuts like the one we took?"

"That's the only stable one we know about," Rendall responded.

"What do you mean by that?"

"This is just a guess." Rendall hesitated a moment. "Grisson, think about what happened when you flew through the mists into God's throne room. Do you remember the path?"

The little angel shook his head. "It didn't seem as if I'd flown very far at all. But I don't think I could find the way again."

"Even if you could remember the exact route you took, it would do you no good. Follow it, and you'd still be underneath the falls, wandering in the mists." Rendall swept his arms wide in a huge gesture. "God's throne room is bigger than any of us can imagine. If it were not far into the mists, don't you think we'd be able to see it easily?"

Grisson frowned. "I never thought about it in that way."

"It very well could be that God creates different shortcuts every time someone is called before Him. The real location of

His throne room might not be anywhere close to the *Place of Becoming.*

The two angels held to the mast a bit tighter as the boat angled steeply. The small craft climbed a wave of light that seemed to rise forever. At its summit, they could see far across the sparkling surface. Colors swirled as the currents of light twisted, flowed, and shimmered throughout the ocean. Light splashed into the air, forming myriads of rainbows.

"Your lessons are complete," Rendall announced.

Grisson whirled around. "Surely you're joking!" He saw his teacher shake his head. "But what about all the formations and exercises I saw the other angels practicing in the cavern? Don't I need to know any of that?"

"I believe God has already provided you with that knowledge. You just don't realize it yet."

Grisson stared at him. "What are you talking about, Rendall?"

Rendall sighed and stood up. He balanced carefully on the deck of the little boat. "Stand up and I'll show you."

Grisson complied, a puzzled look on his face. The moment he got to his feet, however, Rendall lunged at him, an arm aimed at his throat, another levering downwards toward his knees. Before he even knew what had happened, Grisson found himself sweeping the higher arm away with his hands and springing straight up, beyond Rendall's reach.

"What are you doing?" he asked in bewilderment.

"Trying to knock you down," Rendall answered with more calm than he felt. "Now, you try to do the same thing to me. If you can, I'll explain what's going on."

He watched as the little angel settled in front of him. Rendall turned his body sideways, presenting as small a target as possible. He knew Grisson was fast. He'd have to be extra careful.

When the attack came, one part of Rendall's mind noted with dispassion that it had to be easily the fastest he'd ever encountered. But the teacher had readied himself . . . or so he thought. Grisson feinted to his right, then blurred in from the left, angling toward the teacher's lower body. Rendall's reflexes took over and he smoothly brought up his left leg, ready to kick the attacker out of the way. Then, shock! Too late, he realized the second move was also a feint. If Grisson had been fast before, this new move proved almost impossible to follow. He moved back to the right, swept behind Rendall and struck at the back of the lone knee still supporting the teacher. Rendall tried to fly to safety as he fell, but one of Grisson's hands had a wing firm in its grasp. The boat shuddered as Rendall fell heavily to the deck.

"Oh, I'm sorry!" Grisson jumped back, startled at what he'd done. "I really didn't mean to do that!"

Rendall smiled, weariness plain on his face. "Well, at least my theory proved correct."

He motioned for both of them to sit down again.

"Grisson, I've taken self-defense classes for many light cycles. I'm one of the better angels in ability, even though I'm mainly a teacher." His hair waved about, as he looked straight at the new angel. "You've never had a class, never seen a demonstration of how all this works. You didn't even know what I'd intended to do. But you stopped my attack with ease and knocked me down before I could even lay a hand on you."

He looked out across the ocean and shook his head. "I'm not sure why, but God has decided to create you with some unique gifts no other angel has ever had. So, be thankful for what you have."

"What happens now?" Grisson asked.

"Now you begin fulfilling your purpose," the teacher said.

Taken by the current, their boat quickened its pace across the liquid light. After a long while, Grisson managed to speak. "Rendall . . ." he reminded his teacher with reluctance, "I have no purpose."

The tall angel left the cavern and moved slowly into the corridor leading to the falls. His thoughts whirled, confused by the speed of both Grisson's flying and his ability to grasp difficult aerial maneuvers. It just wasn't fair! Since the little angel's *becoming*, Grisson had stunned everyone.

Volthra'an remembered the day of his own *becoming*. The wonder of the Eternal Country had spread out beneath, around and above him in divine splendor. Angels surrounding him had welcomed him into their fellowship. And then . . . the memory of his first encounter with God as he stood on the rocky precipice at the edge of the falls. Love had *enfolded* him completely. A voice whispered in his mind, "My name is LeSage; today I am speaking for God. He says that Volthra'an will be your name forever."

The angel had turned in that moment and announced his name to those watching. "Hail Volthra'an," had come the response.

"Your purpose," continued LeSage, "will be to organize all of Heaven's angels, forming legions, companies and ranks. You will help your fellow angels become prepared for the next Age. God has gifted you with the best mind for organization in all of Heaven. Tell everyone of your purpose, for it will encourage them."

Volthra'an had realized his eyes were closed. Opening them, he once again addressed his celestial audience. "My purpose is to organize all of us. God says this will help bring about the next Age and . . ."

At these words, the angels had begun cheering. And hearing their enthusiasm and happiness, a holy pride had infused Volthra'an's spirit. Life had been wonderful on the first light cycle of his existence.

"No," Volthra'an said to himself. "Let's be honest. Life was good for many light cycles."

He remembered his first meeting with Michael and Lucifer. The two senior angels towered above him, but only gentleness and love shone from their eyes as they looked him over.

"Which one of us should take him?" Lucifer had asked. "If

he's to organize all the angels, he'll have to be working with both of us."

Michael thought for a moment. "I know the angels are equally divided between you and me, but you are the ultimate leader. It seems to me Volthra'an should be under your command. He can help all of us, but since you're responsible, after God, for everything that happens in Heaven, I think this new angel should report directly to you."

Lucifer nodded. "Good point, but I think in actuality he'll have to work as closely with you as with me. So, I'm going to put him under your authority until further notice. That way, when he does have something to report to me, you'll already know and the input from both of you will be that much more valuable." Having made that decision, Lucifer had swung his head around, his long hair whipping about him, and asked Volthra'an, "Do you have any idea how you'll accomplish all of this? Or, am I asking too early in your training?"

Volthra'an smiled as he remembered his response that first light cycle. "I'll begin assessing each of the angels immediately after my training," he'd responded. "They will be divided into sub-groups, with each group having its leader. The sub-groups will be organized into smaller groups, with captains overseeing them. The captains will report to generals, and those generals will then report directly to you." He had been surprised as the words had left his mouth. *Where did all that come from?* He had wondered. "In that way, you'll know what each small group of angels is doing without having to individually talk to each one."

Lucifer's eyes had grown large as he thought about the implications of Volthra'an's plan. "We could have used you many light-cycles before this! You are, indeed, a blessing."

Volthra'an remembered that he'd ducked his head in embarrassment. He knew there was a lot to do, and much he still didn't understand.

"I don't mean to be too bold, but you two should begin choosing your captains and generals while I do the angels' assessments," he'd continued. "I will classify and catalogue each angel's gifts and place them with other angels of different gifts. In this way, every group should be more or less complete in its abilities to carry out God's plan for the next Age."

Michael had patted him on the back at that point. "I agree with Lucifer. Volthra'an, we've been waiting for an angel with your kind of purpose!"

Volthra'an came back to the present. He found himself on the same ledge where everything had begun for the angel with great organizational ability. In front of him, the River of Life roared as it fell majestically from on high. Rainbows formed wherever he looked, brought into existence by the eternal light gleaming through the mists. Spray from the falls glistened on his face and wings, causing Volthra'an to glow even more brightly.

For the first time, none of the beauty moved him. The changes he had made for the angels, though beneficial, were like ashes in his mouth. They no longer mattered.

Alone except for his thoughts, Volthra'an finally gave voice to his deepest feelings. "I don't care about my purpose anymore," he whispered. "I want to be the best flyer in Heaven. I want to be even better than Grisson."

———

In the darkness of nowhere, a disturbance roils the thick blackness. The moaning intensifies, the groaning now more pronounced. Soon . . . soon?

CHAPTER SEVEN

"WATCH OUT! HEADS AND WINGS UP!"

The words, shouted at enormous volume, startled the two angels. Rendall looked around just in time to see a huge boat rushing down upon them. With a sick feeling, the teacher knew he'd never get away in time. The prow of the oncoming behemoth threatened to crush their tiny craft.

Rendall felt himself jerked upwards with tremendous force. In the space of an instant, he found himself dangling from Grisson's arms, looking down upon the crash from an impossibly high distance. Two worried faces peered up at them, as startled as Rendall and Grisson were.

"Are you okay?" Lucifer asked.

"We had no idea anyone else could possibly be anywhere on this ocean," Michael added.

Rendall realized Grisson held him with a trembling grip. He gently disengaged the angel's fingers and said, "Thank God for your quick reflexes!" Together, they floated down to the enormous water craft God had provided for Michael and Lucifer.

The two leaders still looked concerned. "We're so sorry. We never thought anyone else could fly up here by themselves."

Rendall took the lead. "For Grisson, the journey up here constituted no test at all. He even made it dragging me!"

"Stop it, Rendall," Grisson said in embarrassment. "You helped us get here."

Lucifer nodded. "Well, now that you're both here and in good shape, tell me, Rendall, how is his training going? Will you complete it in the allotted time?"

"You might not believe this," Rendall said – a little smugly, Grisson thought – "But I've already taught him everything he needs to know."

Michael looked stunned. "The free fall test?"

"From the top of the cavern; perfectly executed," Rendall purred.

Lucifer looked skeptical. "Come on. No one's ever done that before."

"Ask Stavros. He saw it and actually smiled."

Michael looked stunned again. Maybe it was getting to be a habit. "Stavros *smiled?*"

Lucifer seemed to still be trying to sort everything out. "What about the self-defense classes? There's no way he could have completed those courses by now."

"Aah . . . he didn't need any lessons in that area." Now Grisson thought his teacher sounded a little nervous. What could be happening?

Michael and Lucifer looked at one another and seemed to come to a mutual decision. "Well," Lucifer said, "I guess one of us had better see just how good he really is."

"But Lucifer, you and Michael are the best in Heaven. Surely someone else can test him." Grisson had been right. Rendall was *nervous*!

Determination in his voice, Lucifer stated, "I'll try him first. If he manages to do well, I won't insist on any more training. But I've promised God Grisson will be ready, and I'd hate to tell Him we've both been lax in properly preparing the new angel.

"Don't worry," he added. "I promise to go easy on him."

"Lucifer, that's not why I'm worried." Rendall frowned, unhappy with the turn of events. "I hate to say it, but, frankly, you can't beat him. Michael and you together *might* have a chance. But not alone. That way, it won't be any kind of contest."

There Michael stood, looking stunned again. If he kept looking like that, Grisson thought, his face might freeze in that position. The thought made him grin.

"You think this is funny, new angel?" Lucifer asked.

Grisson coughed, embarrassed. "No, not at all. I . . . . "

"Come on," Lucifer interrupted, motioning to him. "Let's get started with the test." Then he turned to the teacher. "Rendall, we've been wondering why God gave us such a large boat this time. We've never had such a huge craft before. God doesn't provide what's not needed; you know that." He looked around at the spacious deck. "Now we know why this is here. God wants us to test the new angel on this boat, away from prying eyes."

Rendall sighed. "Okay, Lucifer. I'm still warning you, the only way you're going to make this any kind of contest is for the two of you to attack him."

Lucifer nodded. "Sorry, I'm going to have to try this myself to believe it." And without another word the biggest angel in all of creation blurred into action. He threw his wings forward and attempted to block Grisson's vision. At the same time, he stomped down hard on the little angel's foot and sent a huge fist powering toward the same knee.

At least, that's what he *tried* to do. Instead, Lucifer's wings touched nothing, his foot stomped the deck, and his fist hit only air. He turned to see Grisson floating behind him with a quizzical expression. "Sir, what am I supposed to do?" he asked. "I don't understand the rules of this contest."

"Attack me!" Lucifer roared.

Taking the angel at his word, Grisson flew directly behind Lucifer and, before the angel could turn around, kicked him as hard as he could in the back. It was like kicking rock. Lucifer never moved. Instead, he whirled around, concentrated now, to confront his tormentor. Then came a harder kick, but this time it hit his shoulder. Grisson had somehow anticipated Lucifer's move and had used the angel's momentum to further throw him off balance. Lucifer staggered forward. That's when he felt a third kick, this time to the back of his already-slumping knees. He fell face forward on the deck with a loud thump.

Grisson looked on, horrified at what he'd done. Now he was in for it! A strange, choking sound came from Lucifer as he lay there. Rendall rushed to help him, but the mightiest angel in Heaven waved him away. When Lucifer finally managed to turn over, the choking sound turned into laughter, astonishing everyone -- especially Grisson. It bubbled up from Lucifer's chest and sped across the liquid light surrounding them. Grisson imagined his stunned face mirrored how Michael had been looking earlier. "You . . . you're not mad?" he managed to stammer.

"Mad? Why should I be mad?" Lucifer said in good humor. "That's never happened to me at the hands of anyone except Michael." He glanced at Michael, a sly grin on his face. "And even then, it hasn't happened very often." He looked back at Grisson. "Why should I be angry because God has brought into being such a wonderful creation as you? It only makes the Eternal Country a better place."

Grisson sighed with relief.

"My turn now, little one," Michael said.

The sigh turned into a groan. "Do we have to? I don't like doing this to anyone."

Michael's expression softened. "There's nothing to worry about. God has created you with a unique gift. We're just testing its limits to know better how to employ you."

"Well, if you put it that way," Grisson said. "Okay, let's get this one over as fast as possible."

"Your wish is my command," Michael said. And with that, he threw a powerful kick at the little angel. Rendall saw Grisson reach for the foot to bat it aside. The teacher shook his head.

Perhaps this time Grisson had met his match. He was falling for the archangel's favorite move. For as the first foot shot out, Michael moved his wings in a blur. They held him in place so that the other leg could aim at Grisson's head.

Only again, nothing remained for him to aim at. His target vanished in a flash.

Rendall watched as the spindly looking angel dove toward the deck, coming up under and behind Michael. Grisson continued straight up and wrapped his arms around his opponent's wings. Suddenly stilled, the wings could no longer support Michael. Both legs straight out in front of him, Michael crashed to the deck. He looked up to see Grisson hovering just out of reach in front of him, a little smile finally playing around the corners of his mouth.

Michael got up slowly, rubbing his back. "Rendall, Lucifer and I owe you an apology. We should have attacked him together." He continued to rub his "landing spot." "Who would have believed it?"

Lucifer looked pleased with the situation. It seemed as if nothing could destroy his good humor. "Well, this is one of the most interesting experiences I've ever had," he declared. He turned to Rendall and put out his hand. "Thanks for the fine job you've done, and in such a short time."

Rendall ducked his head, as if embarrassed. "To tell you the truth, I didn't do much. God created Grisson with most of these gifts already in place."

"Maybe so," Lucifer said. "But you helped him discover and utilize them." He looked to Michael for confirmation. The archangel nodded in agreement. "What I said still stands," Lucifer continued. "You did a great job . . . ." His eyes widened as a thought struck him. "Since you're so good at fighting, maybe you're also good at solving puzzles!"

Michael and Rendall groaned. "Not that old story again," Michael said.

"It's not old for Grisson," Lucifer replied, unperturbed.

"Besides, maybe Heaven's newest angel can solve the puzzle." He looked at the little angel. "No one, and that includes me, has ever been able to come up with the answer."

In spite of his fatigue, Grisson found himself interested. "What exactly is this puzzle?" he asked.

Michael and Rendall groaned again.

Undeterred, Lucifer pointed above them. "See the mirror image of the Ocean of Light? What is the barrier that's bouncing back its image? And more important – at least to me – is this: what's on the other side?" He continued with his story . . .

———

Michael and I had flown up to the ocean thousands of times over hundreds of thousands of light cycles. Each time, I would find myself glancing at the barrier and wondering about it. In talking with other angles, I discovered no one had ever approached the barrier, touched it or tried to cross it. Even Rendall and Le Sage knew nothing about it. Most angels had the greatest of difficulty even reaching the Ocean of Light. Trying to fly even higher to the distant barrier seemed unthinkable.

The more I looked at what I began calling "God's mirror," however, the more determined I became to learn more about it. So I devised a plan. Early one light cycle, I flew alone to the ocean. But this time, when I landed, I did more than just rest in the boat God provided. After regaining my strength, I cupped my hands in the liquid light and began drinking as much as I could hold. Instead of getting heavier, I found my strength growing enormously!

When I couldn't hold another drop of light, I gathered myself, sprang as high as possible, and began winging my way toward the barrier. Even with the added strength, however, the higher I got, the farther away the barrier seemed. Strong winds pushed against me, trying to force me downward. I used up every bit of the extra energy I had in fighting those currents. But I refused to give up. Little by little, I climbed higher, fatigue pulling at me every wing-beat of the way. Finally, with a last burst of energy, I managed to bump against the mirror. To my surprise, it rippled.

Perhaps I could break through it and see what was on the other side of Heaven!

My strength ebbing fast, I pulled back my fist to try a powerful blow when . . . a seraphim appeared between me and the barrier. It so shocked me I fell several hundred feet before catching myself.

"I have a message for Lucifer from the Almighty One," intoned the seraphim. Two of his wings still covered his eyes. "God commands you to never again attempt crossing the barrier. You must never touch it or try to breach it. The moment you do so, you will be banished from Heaven forever."

With those words, the seraphim disappeared. I gave in to the fatigue, floated back down to the Ocean of Light and have since contented myself with simply admiring the barrier from afar.

———

Lucifer turned from looking at the barrier far overhead. "So," he asked Grisson, "can you solve the puzzle?"

The little angel shook his head. "Sorry to disappoint you, but I have no idea what's on the other side of the barrier."

Rendall smiled. "Lucifer, Grisson doesn't know about the purpose of the seraphim."

"I'm sorry," Lucifer said. "Grisson, I'd love to know what's on the other side of the barrier, but it's evident God has said to leave off trying to find the answer to that puzzle." He grimaced. "So, I'm leaving the barrier alone.

"The true question concerns the seraphim."

Grisson looked at Rendall. "What's he talking about?"

"God's purpose for the seraphim is well known among the angels," Rendall replied. "He has decreed that they will never leave His presence. Not a one of them has ever left the Throne Room since any of us were created."

"I'll take over here," Lucifer interrupted. "It's my puzzle, after all." He grinned at Rendall, but didn't apologize. "There are several questions the appearance of the seraphim brings up. For example, why did God allow the seraphim to leave the Throne Room? How could the seraphim go against his purpose? Finally, biggest of all: does this mean God changes the rules He, Himself, set up for all of us?"

Michael put a hand on Grisson's shoulder. He spoke quietly. "What Lucifer is really asking is if it's okay with God for us to deny our purpose and do what we wish."

"No, that's not it at all," Lucifer said. "I want to know if this is God's way of *encouraging* us to think freely and act independently of our purpose."

Michael shook his head. "That's dangerous thinking, in my opinion. God's instructions to us have always been crystal clear. We are to obey our purpose above anything else. If God decides to change His mind, He will tell us."

"Don't mind them." Rendall waved a dismissive hand at Lucifer and Michael. "They've been arguing about this ever since I can remember."

"It doesn't matter. The answer's still the same," Grisson said. "I have no idea how to solve the questions this puzzle presents."

Lucifer winked at him. "Just keep thinking about it. Your newness is refreshing. You might have a way of looking at things that will give you insights the rest of us don't have. After all," he said, returning to the previous subject, "you defeated the two best fighters in all the Eternal Country."

Michael glanced over at Grisson. Heaven's newest creation looked sad. "Hey, we're not mad!" he said, trying to give the angel some comfort. "Never worry about using your God-given gifts to the best of your ability. You reacted in the way God designed you to react."

Grisson shook his head. "It's not that." He looked at his teacher for help.

"Grisson's worried because he still doesn't have a purpose," Rendall said. "He doesn't know what to do now."

Michael threw a comforting arm around the little angel.

"Don't worry, Grisson. God never makes mistakes. Just trust Him and you'll be all right."

Grisson nodded and the tension eased from his face. "You're right, of course. I needed that reminder. As soon as possible, I'd like to ask you about what I should . . ."

"EVERYONE TO THE THRONE ROOM IMME-DIATELY!"

The four angels looked around, startled to hear LeSage's voice coming from everywhere at once. Rendall saw an exultant expression come across Lucifer's visage once more. "This is it!" he said.

A roar could be heard in front of them. They had reached the edge of the Ocean of Light. As they watched, the light streamed over the edge, falling, falling towards the mists and God's Throne far below. The boat disappeared from beneath them, its purpose completed.

Most angels dropping from the ocean would glide slowly beside the falls as they descended, making sure their wings could control their speed. Because Michael and Lucifer were so strong, they actually dove over the falls and angled downwards head-first, their wings folded behind them in a controlled fall. About a third of the way down, they were startled to see Grisson streak by them, his wings speeding his descent. A bewildered Rendall followed just behind, hanging on to Grisson's foot for dear life.

Things were certainly changing in Heaven, Michael thought.

CHAPTER EIGHT

As he and Lucifer flew through the mists, Michael could see thousands of angels around them. All followed the same twisting pattern as their leaders. The divine compass placed within each would bring them with unerring precision to the Throne of God – and to change forever.

Michael's strength and common sense had long ago made him a beloved and respected leader of the other half of Heaven's angels. His title of archangel bespoke power and authority. But his own personal qualities were what made those under him ready to follow wherever Michael led. Now, however, he wondered just where he'd be leading those loyal followers. Lucifer's purpose might be changing with the new Age approaching. But Michael's new orders, if there were any, remained concealed in the mind of God.

Music, achingly beautiful, began drifting through the mists. It drew Michael and the other angels onward toward the throne. One voice wafted above the heavenly chorus. It soared in wondrous grace as the singer praised the Creator and urged others to do the same. Telsha'in, Heaven's choirmaster, an angel blessed with the greatest voice in Heaven, called all of creation to worship before God. Michael lifted his voice to join the ever-growing symphony of angels singing of their love for God. A glance to his side left him surprised. Lucifer sang not a note. Instead, he flew silently, a strange expression on his face. His wings moved ever faster, as if the big angel could not wait to come before God.

The music grew in volume, the light became blinding in its intensity, and a moment later Michael found himself in the presence of God.

Flying to his accustomed place before God's Throne, the archangel noted with satisfaction the other angels falling into formation as they appeared. In the space of a few moments, Michael could see all his angels were present. Lucifer, beside him, nodded that his contingency had also gotten into place. The last angels to arrive added to the already overwhelming sound of voices raised in adulation, and the music continued to grow more magnificent. Melody coming forth in perfect harmony swirled up from the myriads before the throne, seeking the face of God, its sole purpose for being, its only inspiration. God's love responded. It swept into the center of every being worshiping his Lord.

This is what I live for, thought Michael, to sing, praise and love God.

"Angels beloved by God." LeSage's voice, divinely amplified, filled every part of the vast throne room. Each of the hundreds of thousands of angels could hear as if LeSage stood directly before them.

"All of you have fulfilled, thus far, your purposes in admirable fashion. You give to God much joy."

Michael fell to his knees in thanksgiving, pride warring with humility. The pride stemmed from God's praise of each of them. He had acknowledged a job well done. But the humility remained uppermost in the archangel's mind. He and every other angel in Heaven knew that next to the awesome glory of God, they deserved nothing. As he looked around, Michael saw he was not alone. God's love had driven everyone to their knees because of their great devotion to Him.

No, not everyone had fallen to their knees. Lucifer, alone, was just now beginning to kneel, as if everyone else's devotion forced him to comply. Michael shook his head. He knew his old friend better than that. Surely he'd been mistaken. Michael reoriented himself toward God, where he knew his attention should have been all along.

"Because of your devotion," LeSage continued, "the first Age is complete! The *Age of Preparation* will now give way to the second Age." A spontaneous roar of cheering ripped through the throne room.

When the angels and other celestial beings had quieted, LeSage continued. "God says He cannot, for the moment, give us the name of the present Age. As our part of it closes, we will understand the reason for the mystery. He will, however, give us the name of the third Age. It will be called the *Age of Humans*. These two Ages will eventually overlap, but perform different functions."

LeSage looked down at Stondrin. "And now, curious one, you may ask the question bursting to get out of your mouth."

Stondrin gulped, then gave a tentative smile. "I . . . I was wondering, what are Humans?"

"Humans will be God's next great creation," LeSage announced. "Humans will live in a universe He creates for them."

LeSage looked over at Lucifer and motioned for him to approach. "Many of you have wondered about Lucifer's ultimate purpose. He has led the angels under his charge nobly and with honor. But in the Third Age, Lucifer will begin fulfilling his true reason for existence. As God creates Earth, the home of Humankind, Lucifer will be in charge of guiding the course of the planet and protecting its inhabitants."

Michael could see Lucifer glowing as their Creator spoke of him. The archangel felt a glow within himself, as well. To finally fulfill God's purpose must be a wonderful feeling!

"Humankind will be the Lord's greatest creation." LeSage continued to explain the Third Age. "In some ways, they will be far weaker than you. But their capabilities will also be enormous. Love is God's purpose for creating them -- so that He may love them, and they may love Him in return. All of us, as angels, will serve God in helping them. And Lucifer will guide them to fulfill their destiny of being called the greatest creation of all."

As LeSage spoke, God looked deeply into the heart of each angel. "Remember two things: in serving God and helping Humankind, you will attain more happiness than any of you has ever known. And, above all, remember the Father's love for you."

"Lord?" the voice sounded strangled. Michael could see Lucifer beginning to turn pale. Heaven's most powerful creation clutched his throat, as if the words would not come out. "You see my heart. You know my question."

LeSage turned toward the throne, listening intently. After a time, he turned back to Lucifer. He spoke gently, full of compassion. "Not only does God know your question, He also sees your pain. You may give voice to both of them."

"I . . . I thought we, the angels, were to be God's ultimate creation . . . and . . . I also believed I would be the most powerful of all." Lucifer's body seemed to sag. He grabbed an angel beside him for support.

"Lucifer, God never told you the angels were to be the highest creation. Nor did God tell you that your strength would be greatest among all beings. You have received His love and His blessings since the moment you were created. You have never lacked for anything. The more you have obeyed God, the happier you've become. Lucifer, know this: as you fulfill your destiny, you will be blessed with love, joy, peace and honor. You will be fulfilled even more than you have been."

LeSage paused. Every angel listened intently. They understood the words were for them, as well.

"Know this," LeSage announced. "Everyone who obeys God will ultimately live in peace and harmony forever. But if you do not obey His commands . . ." LeSage paused, and each angel could feel the weight of the Creator's attention upon him. "Your disobedience will cause you never to be a part of Heaven again."

For the first time any angel could remember, complete silence filled the throne room of God. Seraphim, cherubim and angels stood mute before God as the implication of His words sank in.

LeSage continued. "You can avoid this dreadful fate by obeying God's words and remembering His love."

One last time, Michael and the others were overwhelmed with the divine love of God. *I will never do anything that keeps me from the love of my God*, Michael vowed to himself.

Then everything shifted.

Telsha'in, Heaven's choir master, had no idea where the other angels had gone. But he and LeSage found themselves alone in the rock cavern. "What's going on, LeSage?" he asked. "Why have I been brought here?"

LeSage answered his question with another question. "Tell me, Telsha'in, what is most precious to you in all of creation?"

The angel responded without hesitation, "To sing for my Lord and my God."

"Are you sure of that?" asked LeSage.

The angel faltered for a moment. Then he said, "Yes, I'm sure."

"In the time to come, Telsha'in, give careful consideration to God's question and to your response." LeSage looked intently into the choir master's eyes. "God wants you to know it will determine where you spend the rest of eternity."

Michael found himself, with all the other angels, flying near the *Place of First Awareness*. Mists of light showered them with energy. But that was not all: God the Son appeared in the midst of them! Michael shook his head and looked again. God still remained. The archangel had never seen the Creator outside His throne room. He had heard that God the Son created all things, so if he and the other angels were with God, then perhaps . . . .

"Beloved angels!" LeSage flew beside the Lord, his amplified voice commanding everyone's attention. "Since our role will be bound up with Humankind, God thought it only fitting that we accompany Him as He creates the place where they will live."

God the Son drew a line in the air. Where his finger had been, a vertical slash of silver now hung in the air. The Creator slipped through it halfway and stopped. Only part of His body remained visible. "Follow the Lord!" LeSage shouted. Then both disappeared into the silver.

Michael and Lucifer roared as one, "You heard him. Follow the Lord!"

The two angels dove for the line. Michael felt intense cold seep into him, his eyes saw only silver, then he fell through the slash and into . . . nothing.

CHAPTER NINE

None of the angels had ever before seen darkness. As these creatures of light exploded through the slash, they found themselves surrounded by an intense black fog that threatened to suffocate them. Shouts of panic and confusion pierced the darkness as angels huddled together in fright.

"Calm down everyone," Michael shouted. "We have followed our God. He will take care of us. Have faith in the Creator who loves you."

God the Son appeared in the midst of the angels. The light from Him dispelled the darkness in a huge circle, and the angels crowded into that circle of light and safety.

Beside God stood a whitely-glowing blaze of pure power. It seemed familiar to Lucifer, though he knew he'd never seen it before. The Lord gestured toward it, and LeSage said, "This is the Well of Power. Long ago, God created it as a reservoir."

"What does it contain?" Stondrin again! Lucifer smiled as he thought that even fright could not stop the angel's curiosity for long.

LeSage's explanation surprised them all. "It contains the essence of all creation," he said. "We angels were made from this."

That explained why the power seemed so familiar, thought Lucifer. He edged over to the Well, drawn to it and repelled at the same time. He moved his hand toward the opening and–

"Beware, Lucifer!" LeSage's voice cracked like a whip over the assembly and Lucifer snatched his hand back. "God says that you cannot survive as you are if you touch it. You will be changed forever." LeSage's voice softened. "The Well of Power is your greatest danger, Lucifer. God wants you to stay away from it."

Lucifer nodded, but he never looked at God. Instead, his eyes remained fixed longingly on the Well.

"Where is God's choir master?" asked LeSage.

"Here I am." Telsha'in made his way through the ranks of angels to station himself before God. "Gather your choir, Telsha'in," LeSage said. "Prepare them to sing."

As the choir master arranged his singers, God the Son reached into the Well of Power and drew out a massive amount of creative essence. When he released it, the bright substance spread out before him.

"Angels, get behind the Lord," warned LeSage. No one had to be told twice. With so many new events swirling around them, the angels wanted the protection of the Son of God. Lucifer managed to maneuver himself closest to the Well of Power -- just to be able to see better, he told himself.

Again and again the Lord reached into the Well and drew out dazzling power. After what seemed like an entire Age, He finally stopped. The glow from the withdrawn substance stretched farther than even angel eyes could see, illuminating everything. In the place of the darkness that had covered everything in shadow, now only joyous, pure light could be seen.

The Lord looked at LeSage and nodded His head. The angel fairly glowed as he shouted, "Telsha'in, instruct your angels to begin singing!"

The heavenly chorus started softly as God the Son gathered the foundation of the universe into His arms. He shaped it with gentleness, forming the power into a glowing sphere. The ball's huge mass dwarfed the hundreds of thousands of angels watching in awe. But the Creator did not stop His shaping. He continued to squeeze and compress it into an ever-smaller ball. Brighter and brighter glowed the power as it became divinely contained under intense pressure. Louder and more glorious swelled the music as Heaven's most beautiful voices gave praise to God the Son.

The music rose to a crescendo. As Lucifer, Michael and the other angels watched, God compressed the power until its mass could fit in a cherubim's hand. Pulsating wildly, the sphere hung in space before them all, awaiting the Creator's instructions.

The singing stopped.

God the Son paused.

"Lord . . ." Stondrin began. The Creator raised a hand without looking and halted the curious angel.

All watched in wonder as God the Son began to change in form. Gone was the sheen of power that always surrounded Him. His divine nature seemed to shrink. As it did, the darkness advanced, threatening to consume everything in its path. Now only the Well and the compressed ball of power gave light; none came from the transformed Son of God. Barely visible in the darkness, He resembled a small, pure-white creature with four legs. The angels gasped as a terrible ripping sound came from the creature's interior, and God's face twisted in pain. A jagged wound appeared in the white skin, and something red began dripping, dripping, falling out and away toward the pulsating ball, then flowing into it, as if this essence from the Son of God would be part of the new universe.

"Father," God the Son whispered. **"I am willing."**

When the Voice came, it overwhelmed everyone. ***"This is my beloved Son in Whom I am well pleased. Worship Him!"***

Michael and Lucifer led the angels in kneeling before the wounded creature. They did not understand what had just occurred, but knew it must be significant. All lowered their eyes and did homage to their Lord. Telsha'in began to softly lift up a song of praise. After a moment, the others joined in honoring God, singing:

Lord, You, alone, are worthy of our praise;
Your Holiness and Power proclaim You King.
Eternal One, in thanks, our voices raise
To You, Almighty God, our love we bring.

Lucifer knelt before the Lord, confusion roiling in his heart. So far, God had done nothing Lucifer expected. He could not comprehend the Lord's plan either for him or for this Humankind that would soon be created. The white creature also disturbed him. He thought it ugly and, yes . . . *undignified* for the Lord to appear in such a form. Could it be that God the Son had miscalculated on this particular creation?

When Lucifer and the other angels raised their faces, God the Son stood once more before them. Power and divine brightness emanated from Him, infusing everyone with light. The big angel relaxed. Perhaps things were going to return to normal after all.

Yet, still the Creator paused.

Lucifer could see a mixture of sadness and excitement cross His face, as if this particular creation would cause profound sorrow for God, as well as great joy. The Lord turned to look directly at him, perhaps reading his thoughts. For a long moment, he could feel God's eyes boring into him. A thought suddenly shot into Lucifer's mind, *This creation will change me, one way or another, for the rest of eternity.*

Before Lucifer could reflect further, the Creator had turned back to the pulsating ball hanging before Him. As He did, LeSage motioned to everyone, gathering them in as close as possible. He watched The Creator intently, saying nothing until finally the Lord looked at him. LeSage took a deep breath and thundered, **"It is time."**

The Lord swiveled to look at all the angels and nodded once, as if to confirm to Himself that all was ready. Then . . . God the Son *spoke* the first words of creation.

The sphere exploded.

Matter flew toward the angels at a speed that should have flattened them. Instead, protected by the will of God, they watched as the newborn universe moved by and through them. It disappeared into vast distances, expanding at an enormous rate. Suns, planets, galaxies, and nebulae obeyed God's voice and came into existence. As Heaven's choir continued singing, the stars and planets now seemed to echo the song, until all the Universe resounded with praise for God and His great power. The Creator watched everything; nothing escaped His attention. He turned in a full circle gazing far past the angels. **"It is good,"** He said, nodding with satisfaction. Then God the Son motioned once more to His angelic helper.

LeSage flew to Michael and Lucifer. "It's time to move," he said. "Have the other angels follow the Lord once more." The two relayed the instructions to their captains, who passed the information on to the others. What had been one massed group began to break apart, as angels sought out their proper companies. Ranks formed quickly. In a short time, Michael and Lucifer had their troops ready for flight.

The Lord looked at them, making sure each angel was in proper position and watching Him. Michael and Lucifer raised their hands. In perfect formation, the result of long light cycles of practice in the cavern, the angels followed God the Son as He sped through the universe. Solar systems flashed by in the blink of an eye, so swift seemed their flight. Lucifer could not help but admire the beauty and power of God's vision for the universe as they continued onward. He saw masses of matter flung from the original ball of power already beginning to cool and, in some cases, stabilize. It seemed to him that God -- and the angels -- were not a part of "time" as known in the universe. Their flight took them through this creation, but they were not of it.

Eventually, an enormous black hole yawned before them,

sucking all light into its center. The Creator arrowed toward the darkness and plunged into it. Lucifer swallowed hard and motioned for his angels to follow. After a moment's hesitation, Michael did the same. None of the angels wanted anything to do with the blackness before them, but they obeyed their God and their leaders. One by one, the beings of light followed instructions and flew into . . . where, they knew not.

Only a few beats of a wing later, Michael found himself once again beside the Creator. He had the sense they'd somehow traveled vast distances in an instant. Perhaps this black hole doubled as one of God's "shortcuts" He seemed to love to use. Surprised, Michael noticed the Well of Power stationed by one of the bodies God had described as a "planet." He didn't remember God the Son having brought the Well with Him. Yet there it stood, as if waiting for them.

With the other angels forming into companies as they exited the black hole, Michael flew over to Lucifer. "How are you doing?" he asked his friend.

Lucifer shook his head. "Frankly, I'm not sure. I feel . . . off balance. Nothing is happening the way I had imagined it would."

"Why not just sit back and enjoy what God is doing?" Michael suggested. "After all, He has never before let us down. Remember," he added, "God loves us so much that He only wants what is best for us."

God's most powerful angel shook his head again, but didn't answer.

A line of white sped toward Michael. At the last instant, before Michael could even react in surprise, Grisson stopped beside the archangel.

"Where have you been?" Michael asked Heaven's last created angel. Grisson looked nervous. But, come to think of it, he looked nervous a lot. Michael couldn't blame him. Though created but a short while ago, Grisson's life had been one of incredible change.

"I've been sort of hiding in the angels' ranks," Grisson admitted. "When God asks us to get in formation, I'm not sure where I belong." He paused, and then said under his breath, "I don't belong anywhere."

Michael's heart went out to the little angel. He decided he could at least give Grisson a place and a sense of belonging. "God has given me a certain amount of latitude with the angels," he said. "Until now, no one except Lucifer could keep up with me when I fly. But with your creation, I've found more than a match for my speed."

Michael raised his voice a bit, sure that others would hear his next words. "I order you to be my personal assistant. Your place will be by my side at all times, unless God calls you to another job." He looked down at Grisson. The little angel's eyes sparkled with joy.

"Do you understand your new position?" Michael asked. "Do you think you can keep up with me?"

"Yes sir!" Grisson shouted with glee.

"Always stay alert and be ready to go wherever I go. When you are with me, never let your attention flag even an instant." Michael looked over the angel's shoulder, startled. "Lucifer, what do you want with Grisson?" he asked.

When Grisson turned to look for Lucifer, his attention elsewhere, Michael took off. He flew as fast as he could toward a distant star. In but a moment, he had left the other angels and the Well of Power far behind. His huge wings covered vast distances with each stroke. The archangel dove into a still-forming star, turned right upon emerging, and hid behind a small asteroid. Looking around, he could see no sign of Grisson.

"I guess I showed Grisson he'd better be more on guard," he chuckled to himself.

"Why do you say that?" The voice came from behind him. He whirled around and saw the spindly angel grinning at him from no more than a few paces away.

Michael gave a start, but recovered quickly. "Okay, Grisson," he said, his face splitting into that famous grin, "I picked the right angel for the job. You'll do just fine."

He spread his wings and motioned for Grisson to do the same. "Now let's return to the others." So close they almost appeared as one, the two angels sped back toward God and the Well of Power.

"Where's Stondrin?" Michael asked upon return. His gaze swept the ranks of angels. It looked as if someone else was missing as well, but he couldn't be sure.

"We don't know," said one of Michael's captains. "He was here asking me questions only a few moments ago."

Michael ducked his head and allowed a grim smile to cross his face. Everything else might have changed, but Stondrin's ability to ask questions evidently stayed the same! "Never mind," he said aloud. "Grisson, find Stavros for me and ask him to come here."

As the little angel sped away from him, Michael wondered once more where Stondrin could be.

———

The tall, broad-shouldered angel flew in place at the end of his group's line. A few wing spans separated him from the others.

"Psst!"

The angel cocked his head. What was that strange sound?

"Psst! Benla'al!"

He *hadn't* been imagining it. Benla'al twisted this way and that, but try as he might, he couldn't locate the sound's source.

"Benla'al!" came the whisper once more. "Over here, quick!"

The angel could just see the tip of a wing sticking out from behind a large piece of rock not far from his group. Whoever hid behind the rock must have been able to see Benla'al, because the wing tip motioned for him to come closer. When he rounded the corner, Benla'al snorted, "I should have known. You're always up to something, Stond . . . mmph!" Benla'al never completed his sentence, because of a wing suddenly stuffed in his mouth.

Stondrin grabbed the broad-shouldered Benla'al and jerked him unceremoniously into hiding behind the rock. "Ssh!" he whispered "I don't want anyone to know we're having this talk."

Benla'al reached up and took Stondrin's wing out of his mouth. "What are you up to?" he asked, trying to sound a lot calmer than he felt. What he really wanted to do was force Stondrin's mouth open and shove his wing in all the way. Let the inquisitive angel discover the answer as to how *that* felt. "We don't have time to play your games right now."

Stondrin shook his head. "No games; this is serious." He looked to see if any other angel hovered nearby, but only empty space surrounded them. "I have a message for you," he continued in a low voice. "It's from God."

"*From God!*" Benla'al saw Stondrin's shocked face and he brought the volume down. "From God?" he said softly. "Stondrin, even you wouldn't joke about this." He couldn't believe how serious the usually jovial angel looked.

"Listen fast," Stondrin said. "We may not have much time."

Benla'al nodded. The other angel had his complete attention now.

"One part of my purpose is to deliver a message to you. But God expressly told me to wait until the beginning of the second Age. To be honest with you, over the many light cycles since I received my purpose, I had begun to wonder if I would ever be able to fulfill it." Stondrin couldn't stop the smile from appearing.

Benla'al certainly wasn't smiling! "Why would God single me out to receive a personal message from Him at such an important time?' he demanded. "I'm no Michael or Lucifer. I mean, I'm not even a Stavros or a Volthra'an." Something occurred to him. "Wait a moment, Stondrin. Are you sure you've got the right angel? After all, you've been created a long time. Maybe you're confused about names after all those light cycles."

Stondrin shook his head. "We're wasting time." Benla'al had never seen him so serious! "The message is for you, and God said to tell you it is very, very important." Stondrin took a deep breath, said, "These are God's exact words," and began to quote: *"Benla'al, a terrible time may be coming soon. Your dedication will be tested during that time. You may find yourself utterly alone. Stand firm for Me, remember your purpose, and always be assured of My love for you."*

Benla'al's face wore a shocked expression. "What does it mean?" he asked.

"I don't know." Stondrin put a comforting arm on the angel's shoulder. "But God thinks enough of you to warn you. I won't kid you; it sounds like you're in for a difficult experience. At the same time, God decided many light cycles ago that His love would surround you even in your most difficult moments." He pushed Benla'al toward the edge of the rock. "Come on, let's get back in formation."

"I want to remain faithful. No matter what," Benla'al whispered. But Stondrin wasn't sure if Benla'al spoke to himself, to Stondrin, or to God.

"Lucifer!" The angel looked up as LeSage called his name. "The Lord wants you to arrange your legions before this planet."

Lucifer nodded that he understood, then motioned for Stavros. The stocky angel promptly flew to his side. "Remember all those many light cycles you spent drilling with the angels, instructing them in the proper formations for the beginning of the new Age?"

"I certainly do," Stavros replied.

"Put those formations into use now. Our God has commanded it."

"It will be done, Lucifer," Stavros said. In his unique, gravelly voice, Lucifer's number one angel called out instructions to his own leaders. They complied with God's orders, arranging the angels by ranks and companies, filling the space between the planet and a smaller body hanging in space not far away. The many repetitions in practice showed their value in the quickness of everyone's response.

When all were in place, Lucifer flew to his Master's side. The hundreds of thousands of angels nearly filled the void between the planet and its accompanying heavenly body. It looked as if a vast sheet of blinding whiteness hung in space. Lucifer looked them over once more. "They are ready," he said.

The Creator of the universe turned toward LeSage and placed a hand on His spokesman's shoulder. LeSage looked steadily at the Lord, with silent communication evidently passing between the two for several minutes. The angel finally broke the silence, saying, "Yes, Lord, I understand."

God the Son raised His hand and drew another vertical slash in the blackness of space. It seemed to spill silver light from the vastness of Heaven just beyond. Through the opening, angels close by could even see part of the Mists. The Lord looked back at LeSage once more, as if affirming what He'd said earlier, then turned and disappeared through the new portal, presumably going back to Heaven.

LeSage looked somber as he centered himself in front of all the angels. He gestured toward the the new planet and said in a voice loud enough for all to hear, "Before you lies the future home of Humankind. Here is where Lucifer and his helpers will guide Humankind in becoming the greatest creation of all. When this is accomplished, both Lucifer and the race of Humanity will have pleased God, and He will share with them unbroken fellowship."

Some of the angels, Lucifer among them, looked askance at the muddy-brown planet. They wondered how anything good could come from something so ugly.

"Have faith in God, angels!" LeSage said. "The Lord has not even begun to shape this planet into the glorious beauty it will soon become."

LeSage turned once more to face all the angels. "Soon, God the Son will fully create the Earth, with humankind and animals filling it." LeSage narrowed His gaze until Lucifer knew he'd become the focus of the angel's vision at that moment. "But before God begin this process, He wants your angels trained, ready and sure how each of them will help you oversee Humankind. There will eventually be hundreds of millions of humans to look after." LeSage delivered this last part in a soft, but serious, voice.

Lucifer nodded his understanding.

"I'm returning to Heaven with Michael and his angels, while you begin organizing," said LeSage. "I'll leave Grisson here as a messenger. If you need more troops, just send him to Michael." God's spokesman turned to the big archangel. "Lucifer's job, at this point, is the most important of all of Heaven's tasks."

"I understand," Michael and Lucifer said as one.

"If it becomes necessary to return to Heaven, you need only follow this portal."

"LeSage, before everyone departs, may I ask for one other angel?" Lucifer looked through the ranks of angels, trying to spy the tall, clumsy flyer. "If Michael agrees and God does not mind, I'd like to borrow Volthra'an. I know he's gifted in administration and could help me with this task."

Michael nodded in agreement, glad to help.

LeSage turned toward the portal listening to a Voice no one else could hear. After several moments, he turned back. "Tell me, Lucifer," said LeSage, "is this the only reason you want Volthra'an?"

Had he not known better, Michael would have thought fear flared in Lucifer's eyes for a moment, as if God had seen something Lucifer tried to hide. But the powerful angel only shook his head and said, "I really do need him for his gifts in organization."

LeSage held Lucifer's gaze for a moment. Then he nodded once and said, "God will honor your request." Michael flew to the side of LeSage. He wanted to be ready to act on the next instructions. God's spokesman turned to Michael and motioned for him to follow as LeSage flew toward the slash of silver. "It's time to leave here," he proclaimed.

LeSage thrust Himself through the portal and disappeared. Michael motioned toward the gateway and his followers flew to it, ready to leave this universe of darkness and uncertainty. No, Michael corrected himself, not all seemed ready to leave. One angel held back.

"Let me stay here with Lucifer." Intense eyes blazed in the cold blackness of space. "I'm not afraid . . . like those *others*." Shi'intor turned his back on Michael's forces to emphasize his disgust.

"Sorry, Shi'intor." Michael's voice clipped each word. His displeasure showed with each syllable spoken. "God has already made His choice. And it's evident He's not nearly as harsh in His judgment of your fellow angels as you are." Michael motioned once more toward the portal.

"I thought you could make your own decisions, *archangel*." And before his chief could respond, Shi'intor flew away.

Michael shook his head. That one would probably cause him trouble before long.

Floating beside the portal, he gestured for Grisson to come close. "Well, little angel," he said, "for someone without a purpose, you're managing to stay pretty busy." Michael's mouth curled slightly in a smile. "Stay true to God's love for you."

And then he, too, left the universe.

CHAPTER TEN

Grisson turned to see if he could help Lucifer, but Heaven's mightiest angel had already begun to fulfill his orders. His back to Grisson, Lucifer called out, "Stavros, Volthra'an! Council meeting beside the Well of Power."

With the departure of God the Son, the light had gone out of the universe. Save for the glow emanating from the Well, precious little light could be found. The benefit of the distant suns and stars proved negligible, for angels were beings of light, and their natures demanded a divine illumination that could only be provided by Heaven. Lucifer and the others found themselves trying to operate in a dim twilight which made the angels uncomfortable.

Huddled beside the Well of Power, the three angels began planning for the administration of the soon-to-be-created Humankind.

"Are our angels up to this task, Stavros?" Lucifer asked.

The stocky angel wore an uncertain look on his face. "This is not my area of expertise," he admitted. "I can get angels better prepared to fly and defend themselves. But frankly, I don't have the first idea of how to prepare for the coming of Humankind."

Lucifer turned his attention to the other angel. "What about you, Volthra'an? Any ideas?" The tall, thin angel might be the slowest angel in all of Heaven when it came to flying, but all knew of his gifts in organization.

"Let me think for a moment," Volthra'an said. He looked around at the planet, the angels ranged beside it, at the suns and galaxies glowing dimly in the background, as if searching for inspiration. Finally his eyes fell on Grisson and lingered there. "That's it!" he exclaimed. "We need to create more Grissons."

Lucifer snorted. "Volthra'an, I know you'd like to fly like him, but what you're asking for is impossible. And besides, excellent flyers are not going to help us with this problem." "You misunderstand me," Volthra'an said. "Grisson is here right now as a messenger for God. He acts as a conduit from you to Heaven, informing God's servants of your needs. We need to help our angels become messengers just like him.

"You already know how God had me arrange ranks of angels for Heaven. I now believe God was giving us the pattern for this Age. In the same way, I propose a leader for each section of these humans," suggested Volthra'an. "For the moment, be flexible. Find the leaders first, then add other angels underneath their authority as we see how much work each section will have. In that way, you'll have angels watching over every detail. They can report to their captains, who, in turn, will report to their chiefs. Those chiefs, finally, will report to you anything they deem important or cannot handle."

Lucifer mulled over the idea for a long moment, then nodded. "I'm pleased with the idea, Volthra'an. With some refinements, it should work." But a moment later, Lucifer grimaced and a huge sigh escaped his lips.

"What's wrong?" asked Stavros. "The idea does sound like a solution to your problem."

"You're right, Stavros," Lucifer said. "But that's not what bothers me." His eyes swept over and across the several hundred thousand angels under his command. "I just don't like the idea of using great, strong angels like the two of you, as well as all these others, to help a weak creation like Humankind."

Lucifer seemed to look inward, as if he were unaware Stavros and Volthra'an still flew beside him. "Why should we, who deserve to lead, be relegated to service?" he murmured.

He thought for a long moment, and then turned his head to look at the Well of Power. It seemed to beckon him. How he longed to thrust his hands into the glowing Well, withdraw the power, and help the angels become all *he* thought they should be! But God had said . . . . Lucifer's eyes grew big as a realization struck him.

"Angels, encircle the Well of Power," he commanded.

His followers quickly complied, glad to be closer to the only source of light in the vicinity. They crowded together, so tightly packed it looked as if they comprised parts of one immense being of light. Excitement filled the cold vacuum of space. The angels hoped Lucifer would give them more of the precious light they so desired.

"Hear me well," Lucifer said. "I believe the time has come for all of us to become stronger and more powerful than we've ever been." He looked around. Every eye fastened on him. "It is no accident God the Son left us here alone with the Well of Power. I believe it is His intent for us to use the Well ourselves!"

"Lucifer, what are you talking about?" The sharp response came from Stavros. "You heard God say you shouldn't touch the Well of Power."

Lucifer shook his head. "That's not what He said." He smiled. "I know. God Himself said I have a good memory." He raised his voice so that everyone could hear. "God said that if I touched the Well, I would never be the same again. He never forbade me to touch it."

"God also said the Well of Power could be your greatest danger." Stavros refused to give up on what he regarded as an unwise decision.

Lucifer swept the argument aside with an impatient shake of

the head. "Very well. You may be right. But also note God never said *another angel* couldn't touch the Well.

"Since you're so anxious to follow God's Will, Stavros . . . I order you to reach into the Well of Power, take some of its contents, and hand it to me."

A hush fell over the assembled angels. Stavros, for the first time in his life, looked at Lucifer with disdain. "It's not my place to do something like that."

"Stavros, God has placed you under my command. He *ordered* you to obey me." Lucifer's voice turned to cold steel. "I will not say this again: I *order* you to obey me and reach into the Well of Power."

His eyes never leaving Lucifer, Stavros moved next to the Well. He extended his hands. "What I do," he said to the surrounding angels, "I do for my Lord and my God. Not for Lucifer, because I think this is wrong."

The stocky angel immersed his hands in the Well. Pleasure flooded his normally stoic face. But an instant later, the expression was replaced by pain.

Then he screamed.

The sound went on and on, Stavros trying all the while to extricate his hands from the Well of Power. The scream rose in volume. Stavros whipped his head around to look longingly at the silver slash which led to Heaven. His body began to turn liquid, and the angels could see through him. He gave a convulsive shudder, and –

Stavros no longer *was*. For the first time in all of creation, an angel had been *uncreated*.

———

"Please, Stondrin, no more questions!" Michael shook his head in frustration. That curious angel had been peppering him with questions about the recent events from the moment they reappeared in Heaven. Now, gathered around the circle of the *Place of*

First Becoming, Stondrin, Rendall, LeSage, and the archangel tried to piece together, from their own separate experiences, just what had happened in the new universe.

"I just want to know what to call that white creature," Stondrin complained. "That's my last question . . . for awhile," he added in haste. Everyone laughed at the last remark.

Rendall motioned for silence. "The white creature was God transformed," he said. "It looked different to us, but it was God, and so it must stand for something of great importance. Remember, we worshiped Him." Everyone nodded in agreement.

"I wonder how things are going with Lucifer?" Michael asked, changing the subject. "By this time, he should be making some progress in getting ready for the creation of Humankind. I wish I could . . ."

Michael stopped speaking as LeSage rose to his feet. Horror and pain warred for control of his face. The others looked up in alarm. Something dreadful must have just occurred.

"Please let me be wrong," LeSage whispered. "This can't be true. It . . . it's impossible." "LeSage," Michael said urgently. "What's going on? What happened?"

The wise angel stumbled against the cavern wall. Michael reached out to steady him.

"An angel has just been . . . uncreated. He is no more." LeSage bent his head and wept as he spoke the words.

"That's impossible." "Who was it?" "How can this be?" The questions came hard and fast from his friends.

"I don't know how it happened. But Stavros is no longer," LeSage said.

"No longer an angel, or no longer in Heaven? What do you mean, 'no longer'?" Stondrin asked.

"It means we angels can be destroyed." Michael looked as serious as anyone had ever seen him. "We, who thought angels were eternal, are wrong."

"I don't like this Age," Rendall whispered. No one disagreed with him.

———

Beside the Well of Power, shock froze the onlookers. They could not fully comprehend the *unbecoming* of Stavros.

"What happened?"

"Where's Stavros?"

"Why did Lucifer force him into doing something Stavros thought went against God's instructions?"

The murmur grew as angels looked to one another for an answer or at least an explanation of the terrible event just witnessed.

Lucifer, however, raised his head to the heavens and screamed, "NO! I will *not* be denied!"

Before anyone could stop him, Heaven's strongest angel plunged his arms deep into the Well. Pain flitted across his face. He grimaced as he struggled with some unknown force. For a moment, his body began to turn liquid. But Lucifer would not give in. He continued to fight with intensity on holding in place the essence of his being. His eyes closed and he concentrated with all his considerable might.

Lucifer's great will turned the tide of battle in his favor. His body took shape once again. The massive angel opened his eyes and looked around in triumph. He lifted a handful of power out of the Well and held it up where everyone could see. The over-flow streamed down his hands and, instead of falling away into space, disappeared into his wrists and arms. They thickened and bulged with new strength. A peculiar, fearsome expression covered Lucifer's face. The angels began backing away from him as quickly as possible. It seemed anything could happen, and no one wanted to *unbecome* like Stavros.

But further shock awaited them.

Lucifer looked at the power in front of him for a long time, as if contemplating what to do with it. He saw the angels, fright-ened, unsure, not knowing how to react to him. He had to be careful, or he'd lose control of them in the next few moments.

"Do not worry," Lucifer shouted. "I swear that what happened to Stavros will happen to no one else – unless it happens to me." He paused and looked down, apparently in sorrow.

"I feel deep sorrow for the loss of my friend," he whispered. "It is no one's fault but mine." He looked once again at the power before him. "God was right, of course. Because of my actions, I've changed forever."

"And you've changed someone else forever." The muffled voice came from somewhere in the pack of angels. Lucifer ignored it.

"I will not let anyone else suffer from the unknown," he stated. "I, and I alone, must take the next step."

Lucifer placed the power in his mouth and swallowed. A look of ecstasy came over him. Once more, he reached into the Well of Power, drew out some of its contents and ate again . . . and again . . . and again.

As the angels looked on in uncertainty, Lucifer began to change. He had been massive before, but now he towered far above even the largest of the angels. His beauty had always been unparalleled, but now angels wept for joy as they looked at him. The strength that had always been his hallmark now seemed to surge within his body, restless to get out.

Finally, Lucifer stepped away from the Well of Power. He looked around with new eyes that seemed to take in everything at once.

"Creation is so easy!" he exclaimed. "Now I understand!"

But the angels were not listening. A strange sound, somewhere between a moan and the noise rusty gears make when they grind together, began drowning out the huge angel. It grew in volume. The piercing moan rose to a shriek and seemed to come from everywhere at once.

A moment later, Lucifer discovered the existence of an enemy none of his considerable powers could defeat. Formations broke up as the beings of light fled this new enemy. A fine, black mist appeared from nowhere. Filtering through the crowd of angels shrinking from it, moaning and grinding, the mist made its way inexorably toward the Well of Power and Lucifer. Though darkness filled this universe, the still-blacker mist stood out starkly. Even the Well of Power could not illuminate it. When it reached Lucifer, the mist began moving in an ever-smaller circle, as if trying to surround and entrap him. At first, Lucifer looked down at the puny invader in disdain. He smiled lazily and reached out a hand to bat it away. But when he touched the mist, a look of agony came over his face and Lucifer snatched his hand back.

Taking a new tack, the big angel turned his huge wings toward the mist and, moving them rapidly back and forth, tried to blow this new enemy away. Instead of repelling the mist, however, the wings seemed to draw it like a magnet. Lucifer screamed after a moment. The other angels were horrified to see holes appear in his wings, where the black droplets had burned through their attacker.

The mist continued to spread. Head, shoulders, wings, legs, everywhere the black droplets touched him, Lucifer screamed in pain. Huge welts began appearing on his body, turning red and oozing a foul, black, thick liquid. The blackness seemed to gather in a clot near his mouth and nose, as if trying to seek entry.

"Someone help me!" Lucifer moaned. "God, please deliver me!"

"Lucifer, your request has been heard," spoke a voice that may have belonged to LeSage.

The angel looked up, relieved, and disappeared.

Deprived of its prey, the black mist grew lighter in color. It turned and began flowing toward another group of angels. The rate of speed allowed the droplets to encircle them and cut off all hope of escape. They shrieked in terror. No one had ever had to face such an enemy before. Nothing in their training had prepared them for this. But, even as they began to lose hope, the

Well of Power pulsed once and a stream of bright light shot out from it, blinding everyone. When they could see again, the black mist was no more.

Grisson wasted not a moment. The fastest reflexes in all of Heaven galvanized his wings. He gave not a word of explanation to any of the other angels, but exploded in flight, hitting the silver portal at full speed and leaving behind this universe that, for him, held only sorrow.

CHAPTER ELEVEN

Had Grisson, Stondrin and the others been there when Lucifer appeared before God's Throne, they would have gasped in surprise. Heaven's mightiest angel now towered over everything and everyone, save God. Next to Lucifer, even the Seraphim appeared no bigger than cherubim. The powerful angel could have broken them with his hands, if he'd wished.

Had other angels been in the throne room at that moment, they would have also wondered if the light dimmed a bit with the entrance of Lucifer. It seemed as if a pall had been cast upon everything, causing the brilliance of that Holy Place to shine less. Only God remained unaffected by the arrival of His great angel.

For Lucifer, however, the opposite seemed true. A plethora of sensations hit him upon his entrance. His body healed. The black ooze dried up. The welts disappeared. But the pain of the throne room's light burning into his eyes overrode everything else. It felt as if hot coals were being thrust against him, and it caused Lucifer to fling up an arm in a self-protective gesture.

"My eyes!" he cried. "Why have you made the light so bright?"

"The light is as it has always been," LeSage said, appearing beside Lucifer. "It is you who have changed."

Lucifer crouched before the throne, shielding his eyes and, as best he could, his mind. He knew God was examining him, looking for internal changes, as well as those external ones anyone could see. He could feel, with his new power, the probe of God's Mind. He sent out a tentative probe of his own, trying to learn more about God's power. Apprehension filled Lucifer on one level. On another, however, he thrilled at the thought of understanding how to increase and better use power. It fascinated him, called to him, drew him. As he probed further, God said nothing. Could it be God didn't know of Lucifer's recent actions?

Suddenly, the angel forced his face to remain impassive and his demeanor calm. With his fresh insights into creation, Lucifer believed he could tell God's reservoir of strength held only a fraction more than his.

"God demands that you explain your actions, Lucifer," said LeSage.

The angel felt panic rising in his throat. He'd been found out! But then he realized God spoke of the events at the Well of Power. He knelt before the throne and assumed the position he'd always taken, as if nothing had changed.

"I'm sorry about Stavros, Lord," he said. "I thought you wanted us to use the Well of Power to better prepare ourselves in administering Mankind." There, make it God's fault!

Lucifer kept his head bowed, placed a block in front of his emotions with his newly found power, and hoped that God could not read them. He continued, "I only wanted to try out the power on myself, to keep the other angels from being destroyed." His voice dropped lower as he tried to act concerned. "I couldn't put any more angels in danger. And I didn't try to create anything. After all, that is Your responsibility alone." Maybe sincerity would work.

"Oh, but you did create something, Lucifer." LeSage's voice

crackled with energy, reflecting the anger of Almighty God. The Seraphim fled before its force, leaving the two angels alone with God in the glorious infinity of the throne room.

"The black mist that almost destroyed you can be attributed to your wrong choices. You brought it into existence." LeSage trembled as he spoke the words.

Lucifer looked up, surprised, still shielding his eyes against the light. "What is it, Lord? How could I have created it?"

"Lucifer, you delude yourself." As LeSage spoke the words, compassion filled God's face -- compassion and anger. "God knows that you believe your power is now great. But you understand so little about what is happening. The Well of Power is *God's* creation. It makes you stronger, and so you think to challenge Him. What you perceive as a limit to His power is, in reality, as far as God allows you to see. If He can create the instrument that makes you more powerful, don't you realize He's also capable of stopping you, no matter how great you become?"

Lucifer still knelt before God. Shock and fear immobilized him. God knew everything; he could do nothing to escape. Doom awaited him.

"The black mist is called *Sin*." God's message through LeSage rained down upon him. "You brought it into being when you thought of disobeying God. If you're not careful, your desire for more power will consume you like the black mist attempted to do."

The angel looked up. A small flame of hope began to burn within him. "You . . . You're not going to destroy me for what I've done?" he asked.

"Lucifer, you know God never destroys. He creates. The only way you can be destroyed is to do it yourself."

Lucifer jumped to his feet in exultation. "Thank you, God, I . . ."

"There is more God wants you to know," LeSage continued. "The sin you created and brought into the world has the capability of touching every one of Heaven's inhabitants. And it can touch you again." God's eyes blazed with a Holy light as LeSage spoke the next words. "Lucifer, remember how it burned and hurt. If you choose to act against God, the sin will become a part of your very being. It will push you away from God. It will destroy you. Sin will cause you more pain than you ever thought possible."

Lucifer couldn't believe what he heard. "You're not going to destroy me for what I've done? You're giving me another chance?"

"Remember what God has commanded," Le Sage said. "You have not yet sinned, for you did not understand completely the consequences of your actions. Now, however, you have been warned. Do not touch the Well of Power again. If you do so, temptation and destruction stand waiting to consume you. Stay true to the purpose for which God created you."

He doesn't have the power to destroy me, Lucifer thought. I've grown too powerful for Him.

"God is sending you back to the Well of Power."

Lucifer looked up in surprise. He would never have expected that. Was God blind to what His strongest angel could do, once he returned to the source of creation?

"Remember, this time God is giving you a direct order. Never touch the Well again. In the moment you touch it, you will begin to die . . . forever. Gather your angels and bring them back to Heaven. Once returned, God will give you your next instructions."

God waved a hand, and Lucifer disappeared.

———

Michael and the others looked up as Grisson flew through the portal and landed beside them. They surrounded the spindly angel, asking questions about Stavros and his *unbecoming*. He ignored them all and turned toward the Mists of Light. His hands stretched out almost of their own volition, as if trying to embrace every bit of available light and store it within him.

"How can anyone enjoy being away from this wonderful light?" he wondered. Then, with a long sigh, he turned to his friends. "It's good to be back in the Eternal Country once more."

"LeSage told us something distressing about one of the angels," Stondrin blurted out. "Surely what he said can't have happened!"

Grisson sighed once more. He moved into the cavern and sat down on one of the stone outcroppings. The others followed. Michael leaned against the adjacent wall; the others sat on the cavern floor.

"Grisson?" Stondrin said it with gentleness this time.

"Yes, it's true," the little angel said, bowing his head in sorrow. "Stavros is no more. Lucifer forced him to touch the Well of Power, even though he didn't want to." And continuing, he related everything that had occurred since Michael and the others had left the new universe.

When Grisson finished the terrible story, silence settled on the group. Heaven, other angels, even their future – all seemed changed forever. Since the beginning of their existence, everything in Heaven had remained the same. They had assumed events would always continue more or less as they had before. Now, they struggled to keep up with the almost constant change thrust upon them in the last few light cycles.

Michael pushed himself away from the wall and looked around at the others. "How could Lucifer think of doing such a thing?" he asked. He shook his head in frustration. His friend's actions of late were incomprehensible to him.

"What does he look like now?" asked Rendall.

Grisson flew to a height that forced everyone, even Michael, to look up so see him. "Lucifer's at least this tall," he said. "Plus, he's stronger and much more beautiful than before."

"Why would he do this?" Michael wondered. "Lucifer's

already the biggest, strongest, most powerful angel in all of Heaven."

"But he's not as powerful as God," LeSage pointed out. "Maybe he wants to be."

Michael thought about the other angels in Heaven. They had no idea what was transpiring in the new universe; that ignorance could conceivably be their doom. Someone had to make these innocent beings of light understand that no one could touch The Well of Power and live.

As the implications of the potential carnage hit him, Michael wheeled about and rapidly began walking away from the others. "You may be right," he called back. "In any case, we owe it to the other angels to let them know about what happened to Stavros. I'll tell those in the cavern the news. Then I'll dismiss them to fly throughout the Eternal Country to warn everyone else."

But he never got there.

As the archangel rounded a corner and disappeared from the view of his companions, he found himself in the throne room of God. No summons to respond to this time; no path to follow. One moment Michael walked along the cavern path, the next moment, Seraphim surrounded the angel and God confronted him.

He began to kneel before the One he loved more than life itself. But before he got half-way down, Michael felt a Hand gently pull him back upright. "Lord . . .?"

"No questions, Michael." LeSage whispered. Even the seraphim were unaware of the message. "You have always known your purpose. But you've wondered when you would be allowed to fulfill it."

LeSage paused, and Michael's heart began to race.

LeSage placed his mouth as close to Michael's ear as possible. The archangel had to strain to hear him. "When you hear these words: *'What's wrong with everyone having whatever they want?'* it will be time to take a stand for what is right and defend God. The one who speaks those words will be your enemy."

The angel bowed his head. "It is an honor to have such a purpose and responsibility," he said.

"At that moment," LeSage continued, "you will be given certain powers. Be ready to use them."

The throne room began to grow transparent. LeSage's voice sounded farther away. "Tell no one of this conversation until the moment you begin fulfilling your purpose and using your powers. Be faithful to God's love, Michael. Be faithful . . ."

CHAPTER TWELVE

Stondrin slapped the wall of rock in frustration. Michael had disappeared, as had LeSage. "What is going on?" he demanded to no one in particular. "I'm ready for action, but I have no idea what to do." Rendall raised a finger and started to speak, then stopped immediately. Michael and LeSage appeared in their midst. But the sudden appearance hadn't stopped Rendall; instead, a Divine Summons compelled every angel to listen . . . except for one.

Grisson saw heads whip around to look toward the Mists of Light. For several long moments, silence reigned as every angel – save for him – listened to what Grisson assumed was a divine Voice. Finally, Stondrin, Rendall, Michael, LeSage, and the others said as one, "I understand and will obey."

The little angel wanted to ask what they had heard, but no one offered an explanation. Grisson decided to remain quiet. He didn't want to do or say anything that would make him stand out from the others again. He already felt guilty about the unbecoming of Stavros.

Around the Well of Power, the angels discussed what their next plan of action should be.

Some pushed for going back to Heaven. Others insisted they wait for their leader to return.

"I don't like the darkness of this universe." Volthra'an grimaced as he took in the planet beneath him "Michael is the one I answer to, anyway. I'm going back to Heaven."

"Do that, and you'll never become the fastest flyer of all the angels." The words came drifting down, accompanied by a gigantic, breathtakingly beautiful angel. Volthra'an and the others watched Lucifer glide away from the silvery portal. He paused before them for a moment, aware of the reaction his presence caused.

Dalsa'in, one of his captains, asked, "What happened to you?" The last time they'd seen Lucifer, his body suffered from welts and burns. Now, that terrible event seemed never to have occurred.

The huge angel moved next to the Well of Power. He placed a proprietary hand upon it and motioned for quiet. The angels bunched closer, eager to hear what he said.

"My faithful followers," Lucifer began, "I have uncovered an important secret God has been trying to keep from us." He paused for a moment, wanting to be sure he had everyone's attention. When all eyes finally focused on him, Lucifer continued. "We have grown too strong for God to control!"

Murmurs and shocked whispers shot through the assembled group.

Lucifer waited until they had run their course. Then he said, "I believe God is creating Humankind to keep us in servitude. He is afraid we will discover the true extent of our powers."

"Do you realize what you're saying?" The broad-shouldered Benla'al stepped forward from the group. He made his way toward Lucifer. "You are doubting God!" he said. "If you continue in this way, He'll be forced to destroy you."

The angel had to tilt his head back to see Lucifer, but no fear touched his eyes. Benla'al thought only of his love for God. "If you think God doesn't have the power to destroy all of us with a word, you're deceiving yourself. He created us. He, Himself, gave us our power. We exist because He wills it."

Lucifer looked down at the angel, a contemptuous sneer on his face. "You are a little being with little understanding of anything. I believe we are in the process of growing beyond what God originally intended. We -- or, at least *I*-- have the capacity to become as powerful and as majestic as God."

Murmurs and disbelieving scoffs greeted these words. Lucifer turned to the rest of the onlookers. "You require proof? I will give it to you!

"Hear me well, angels. I have a direct order from God: I must not touch the Well of Power. He has said if I ever take from the Well of Power again, I will be destroyed."

Lucifer raised his voice, until the universe resounded with his shout. "I defy you, God. Destroy me, if you can!"

A gasp went up from the angels and they instinctively pulled away from Lucifer, fearing his destruction would spill over to them. They watched in horror and dread as Lucifer plunged his hands into the Well of Power and withdrew a handful of creative essence. He held it up toward the silver slash leading to Heaven. "Here I am, God! I have disobeyed you! I repeat: destroy me . . . *if* You can!"

The huge angel screamed with all his might, "I *will* be like you, God. And I will rule in *your* place!"

A thunderous wail ripped through all of creation. Its power caused the angels to cover their ears and shudder. The universe convulsed once in a mighty tremor. All light fled from the stars, leaving them in total darkness.

Then the terror began.

"Come on, Grisson. Wipe that nervous look off your face." Michael eyed the spindly angel with concern. "Surely you don't feel responsible for Stavros?"

Grisson refused to meet his eyes. "I was there," he said. "I should have done something, anything, to try and stop what happened. But I watched in silence, instead of acting to save him."

"So you knew what was going to happen in advance?" Rendall had begun using his teacher's voice.

"Of course not," Grisson responded, unsure where the conversation might be going.

"Did you believe Lucifer to be the angel God had placed in charge of everyone?"

"Well . . . yes," Grisson admitted.

"Were you close enough to stop Stavros and Lucifer?" Rendall was unrelenting when he saw the answer to a problem.

"No. I stayed behind all the other angels, ready to return to Heaven if Lucifer needed me to report a problem." The tension began easing in Grisson's face. "I see what you're saying, Rendall. I guess I just feel regretful. How I wish I could've stopped what happened and changed the outcome!"

"We all feel like that, Grisson." Michael put a comforting hand on the little angel's shoulder. "But you can't take responsibility for every bad thing that happens."

Grisson nodded. He looked around at the group of angels he had come to realize were his friends and smiled. "How about helping me out with another problem?"

Stondrin groaned. "Why can't you just have one problem at a time like the rest of us?" he asked.

"Seriously," Grisson said, "I'm not sure if God wants me to stay here or return to the Well of Power. I don't know where Lucifer is."

But what happened next rendered Grisson's question moot and served as a prelude to unimaginable suffering.

The light went out of Heaven.

Only so many angels could crowd into the circle of light made by the Well of Power. Those on the outskirts flailed about in the darkness. Panic ensued. Shouting erupted. And over everything else, a scraping, grinding sound could be heard. Screams and moans began as angels tried, without success, to escape the black mist that attacked everyone. The smell of burning angel skin and the black mist's odor of decay combined to make a cloying, nauseating stench that clogged their nostrils and caused them to gag.

"God, help us," someone called. But God did not answer.

Instead, the huge figure of Lucifer could be seen flying through the darkness. He aimed for the mist, as if the lack of light bothered him not at all.

"Come to me!" he called in a loud, commanding voice. The black mist stopped its rending of the hated beings of light. Bits of wings floated about, ash-tinged. "Come to me!" Lucifer called again.

Turning from its prey with reluctance, the mist saw who beckoned. It abandoned the others and flew directly at the powerful angel. He let it advance and settle on him. Some of the angels shouted a warning to Lucifer, but he held up a hand to stop them. He wanted everyone to understand his new, incredible power.

The mist pulsed as it swarmed over and around him. The black droplets surrounded him in an instant and covered his body. The shrieking, grinding sound stopped. In its place, a soft purr rose up from the black droplets, as if they had finally found their home. Lucifer, for his part, showed no sign of pain as the deadly, sinuous mist writhed on his skin. Indeed, he seemed to revel in it.

After a moment, Lucifer opened his mouth and inhaled with all his might. The black droplets left his skin and were sucked into his mouth. He swallowed.

And in an instant, the terrible mist had disappeared.

Lucifer floated before them all in the darkness and dim shadows. A terrible smile twisted his features. He looked at his followers and said, "As you can see, I'm still here."

The brilliant, glistening light of the Eternal Country was, for a moment, no more. The angels in the cavern huddled together for support. In the almost palpable darkness, a cry of pain could be heard.

"What is that?" The voice, panic tinged, asked the question on everyone's lips.

"Our God is weeping!" said LeSage.

This statement alarmed the angels even more than did the darkness. The sound of divine sorrow went on and on. The darkness seemed to deepen. Someone could be heard stumbling about. Then a "thud" sounded and Stondrin cried out in pain.

"Everyone sit down and be still," Michael ordered.

Grisson didn't know what the others were doing, but he decided to obey. The little angel sat down and leaned a tired face on his knees. He had never experienced the complete absence of light before, and it frightened him. Even the brief darkness of the black hole could not compare with this. Grisson wondered what it would be like to know you had to spend the rest of eternity in such a darkness. He shuddered.

Grisson forced his thoughts away from such a depressing subject. The love he'd experienced in God's throne room flooded his memory. Those thoughts relaxed and calmed him. Meanwhile, he could tell the crying was becoming fainter. Then it died out completely, as if the mourner had left the Eternal Country behind.

Slowly, slowly, the light returned.

Grisson could see Stondrin standing by the cavern wall, rubbing his head. "I got turned around and went the wrong way," the angel admitted.

"Where were you trying to go?" Grisson asked.

Stondrin pointed to the entrance. "Outside. I figured there would be more light out there." He looked around and tried to get his bearings. "But I was wrong. Now I can tell that I'd been looking straight at the entrance and couldn't see it. The light must have gone out all over Heaven."

Michael motioned for everyone to gather around him. "This

has to do with Lucifer, somehow. We're going to have to get instructions from God."

"We can't!"

The words came from LeSage.

"What do you mean?" Michael demanded. "Our Lord knows what needs to be done. He'll have a plan."

LeSage shook his head. "No, you're wrong." A vacant stare had settled in his eyes. His wings drooped in dejection.

"Get hold of yourself, LeSage!" Michael ordered. "This is no time to panic. I'll drop down into the mists and begin flying toward God's throne. He'll guide me and . . ."

LeSage still shook his head.

"You'll never find Him, Michael. He's gone."

"Gone!" Stondrin squealed, his eyebrows raised to their questioning height. "How can God be gone?"

LeSage tried to explain. "From the moment of my creation, there has always been an open line between God and me. It . . . it's like an invisible string running between the two of us. No matter where I go, I can always sense it." He looked around to see if the others understood what he was saying. "That's how I can tell you about what's happening in Heaven. God uses that line to communicate with me when He wants to deliver a message to all of you."

He forced himself to look squarely at the stunned archangel. "Now for the first time, that connection is gone. God has severed it."

"What does this mean?" Rendall wondered aloud.

Michael took a deep breath and let it out. "It means we're on our own," he said.

CHAPTER THIRTEEN

The five angels walked together toward the ledge and the *Place of First Awareness*. No one spoke, though all eyes focused on Michael. LeSage stumbled along and allowed Stondrin to lead him. But Michael strode with a firm pace, a plan of action already forming in his mind. His determination encouraged Grisson. Perhaps all wasn't lost, after all.

Heaven's newest angel shook his head as he thought. He didn't see how he could do anything that would make the least bit of difference in the outcome. God had not even trusted him enough to give Grisson a purpose. Perhaps God had suspected this would happen and had made sure Grisson could not betray Him. Or perhaps the Lord wanted to minimize the damage Grisson, in his ignorance, might cause. Without warning, panic beat against his chest and the little angel felt tears flood his eyes. He had no business being here. The others surely could see that. Why, right now the others were probably wondering why he was even—

"What do you want us to do, Michael?" Rendall's question interrupted Grisson's thoughts. The group had emerged from the tunnel and now stood on the ledge where Grisson first saw

Heaven's light. The River of Light bathed them in a rainbow of colors as it plunged toward the rocks far below.

Michael gathered the others close to him and lowered his voice. The roar from the Mists of Light would drown out his words to anyone but those in the immediate vicinity. "I need some spies," he said. "None of us knows what Lucifer is up to. And if we're going to stop him, somehow we have to obtain information on his actions."

He turned to Grisson. "I think this will be a dangerous mission, but I need you." The little angel paled, but still nodded his head. Michael smiled and placed a comforting hand on his shoulder. "No one in all of Heaven can out-fly you. If Lucifer or any of the others catch sight of you, that speed should be enough to get you back here and to safety."

Michael's eyes swept the rest of the group. "Unfortunately, Grisson still doesn't know all of the angels. I need someone to go with him and help interpret what he sees." He could see fear in everyone's eyes as he explained the situation. But to their credit, no one looked away or refused to go. "As you've no doubt already figured out, Grisson's speed won't save you. If you're seen, you may well be caught . . . ." He hesitated, unsure of how to continue. Could he really let one of his angels be put in a situation that threatened their very existence?

"I must tell you all the truth. There is a strong probability that anyone taken prisoner by Lucifer will suffer the same fate as Stavros. You may be *uncreated*."

Rendall took a step forward. "I'll go," he said. No hesitation, no trembling.

"Are you sure?" Michael asked. "You have to understand the danger involved."

Rendall nodded. "The danger exists for anyone who goes. But I'm the logical choice. Grisson and I know each other. I understand how he thinks. And since I provided his education, I'll be better qualified to fill in any gaps that still may exist."

"I thank both of you," Michael said. He paused a moment to

compose himself. "It's wonderful to have friends who are willing to risk everything for God." As Michael said "friends," Grisson looked startled for an instant, then his face lit up with pleasure.

Michael explained the rest of his plan. "Stondrin, fly into the mists and tell all you encounter to meet me in the cavern as soon as possible. LeSage!" Michael's voice sharpened. The angel roused himself a moment from his stupor. "I need for you to shape up and quit feeling sorry for yourself. You're not helping God or anyone else with all the moping about."

LeSage raised his head, and Michael could see his eyes blaze with anger. Then the angel nodded once, his mouth curved in a little smile, and he straightened his shoulders.

"Fly to the cavern and tell everyone there to remain until I return," Michael ordered, but in a gentler tone. "I'll fly to the top of the Falls and announce, as loudly as possible, there is a convocation in the cavern. Between the three of us, everyone should receive the news."

Stondrin and LeSage took off at once to do their leader's bidding, leaving Michael alone with Rendall and Grisson. He placed an arm around each of them and walked them to the ledge's precipice. The portal into the universe hung before them. None knew what a leap through that gateway might hold for them in the darkness beyond. The unfolding events made it look sinister and uninviting. But their love of God and commitment to their purpose moved them inexorably forward toward the unknown.

"Be careful, both of you," Michael said. "Float out of the portal and put yourself on the other side of the smaller body of matter closest to the planet. In the darkness, no one should see you."

Grisson and Rendall nodded somberly.

"As soon as you've discovered what Lucifer is planning, come back here. I'll have a lookout stationed by the portal who will come get me from the cavern. Make sure you report to no one but me."

Michael stared hard at them, willing them to return safely. "Don't take any chances." He thumped both of them on the back. "I've grown kind of fond of both of you."

"We'll be back," Grisson answered.

Rendall simply said, "Goodbye, Michael."

The two angels spread their wings and glided toward the portal. They decreased their speed to a crawl and disappeared into the universe.

Would it be the last time they ever saw Heaven? Michael wondered.

CHAPTER FOURTEEN

After Lucifer's victory, ragged cheering could be heard from the broken ranks of angels around the Well of Power. He raised his hands in triumph, acknowledging the praise. But as he examined his troops, Lucifer grew serious. He had not realized the extent of the devastation caused by the black mist. Dalsa'in, Volthra'an and the other captains tried to maintain some order, but their efforts proved largely ineffectual. Not only were the troops decimated, their morale had fled. Instead of flying proudly around Lucifer, their leader, they cowered in fear and confusion. He needed courageous warriors, not cowards. Something had to be done, and soon.

"Back in formation, all of you!" he commanded.

The angel troops limped into a semblance of order. Some of them hunched over, nursing wounds. Others struggled to maintain their position, crippled by wings with huge rents in them. All wondered how they could heal without the power of the River of Light.

"Those of you who have suffered harm from the black mist, look to me!"

The wounded angels gazed into Lucifer's eyes and gasped at what they saw. Heaven's most powerful angel no longer had flecks of gold floating in his irises. Now they resembled lumps of coal. His pupils, however, were perhaps the most unsettling of all. Where silver used to gleam from within, now a flat blackness emerged.

As they watched those eyes, Lucifer dipped his hands into The Well of Power. He carefully held a handful of power above his head and gestured for the wounded to draw near. Then Lucifer scattered minute bits of the glowing essence on those angels harmed by the mist. Several of them flinched at this new invader, but the reaction was one of astonishment, not fear. A bright glow blinded everyone for a moment. When it subsided --

"Look!" an angel marveled. "My wounds are healed!"

"And my wings," said another. "There are no holes in them!"

"No pain. The hurting is gone!"

Cheering rose from the group again. This time, however, it seemed as if everyone joined in proclaiming Lucifer's power. They had seen the terrible effects of the black mist erased because of their leader.

"I have healed you all." Lucifer felt pleased with himself.

"No, not all."

He whipped his head around. A feeble Benla'al hovered beside The Well of Power. Half of his face was missing, burned away by the black mist. The remaining half had turned an angry red and oozed a foul-smelling, black substance. One wing dangled precariously, threatening to snap off because of charred flesh. The pain must have been horrendous. But Benla'al still managed to look defiant.

"Why do you refuse my gift?" Lucifer asked. His kind tone made Benla'al's refusal of help seem so unreasonable.

"Don't put up with the pain any longer. It's senseless!" one of the angels urged him. "You've changed, Lucifer," Benla'al explained, ignoring the other angels. "Your eyes are black. They reflect the darkness in your heart. The black mist no longer harms you because you and it are now the same."

Lucifer seemed unconcerned by the charge leveled at him. "I

admit it," he answered. "I have become what God calls 'Sin.' Now the darkness is more comfortable for me than is the light." He raised his voice so that all could hear his next words. "But what is sin? Isn't it nothing more than disobeying God?"

Some of the angels backed away from him at these words. He raised his hands in placation. "Continue to listen for a moment." A smile, beatific and innocent, appeared on his face. How could anyone doubt the rightness of the words spoken by someone of such beauty and charm?

"I've already told you how God knows we are almost as strong as He is. And I've revealed that Mankind is nothing more than a ploy to keep us in slavery forever. God doesn't want us to grow and learn about ourselves."

He swung his head around to look at Benla'al once more. "I have defied God. He said that in the moment I sinned, I would die. Yet here I am!"

Lucifer moved closer to Benla'al. "I give you one more chance. Will you let me heal you? After all, what can you lose -- except a lot of pain?"

The wounded angel struggled to push the pain away so that he could marshal his thoughts. Lucifer's presence nauseated him. He backed further from the big angel and tried to get some space between the two of them. When he realized Lucifer, moving ever closer, was forcing him away from the Well's light and farther into the darkness, he stopped. Benla'al refused to move a wing's length more. Here is where he would make his stand.

"God has never disappointed me," Benla'al said in a loud voice. "He created me – all of us – when He didn't have to. His love has been the greatest gift anyone could give me." Some of the angels nodded in agreement as he said this. Lucifer wore a look of displeasure. The spotlight of attention had moved from him to another.

"Whatever happens, I will not submit to another – even you, Lucifer. You are mighty, but your power has exacted a horrible price from you. To become stronger, you have sacrificed a relationship with God."

Benla'al choked as a wave of nausea rose in his throat. He ignored it and continued. "The black mist you've thanked Lucifer for destroying did wreak great pain upon us all. But remember: it was Lucifer, himself, who first made it come into being through disobeying God's Will."

More of the angels nodded their heads. Some muttered in low tones to one another and looked at Lucifer with less than love in their eyes. Lucifer knew he had to stop Benla'al before things got out of hand.

"Enough of this," the angel of darkness said. "Will you follow me, Benla'al, and allow me to heal you? You've seen what I can do."

Benla'al raised his head and Lucifer could see derision in his face. "You're not God," the wounded angel stated. "You're just a pretender who's gotten too big for his wings!"

"*Enough of this!*" Lucifer repeated, roaring in anger. "If you will not be healed . . . ."

Lucifer opened his mouth. Shrieking, grinding, the black mist roiled forth. The angels cried out and fled from Benla'al's presence. They needn't have worried, however. The mist's goal was the wounded angel, alone. Like an arrow to the bulls eye, the mist flew toward its intended victim. Benla'al tried to flee, but his weakness worked against him. In an instant, the black droplets covered him completely. Pearl-like gobs of silver began oozing from his pores, pushed out as the mist burrowed into his body. Huge gouges appeared in his skin. He listed to one side, drifting as his wings burned and dissolved. The other angels knew the pain must be unbearable, but Benla'al refused to utter a word.

Louder grew the noise of shrieking and grinding. Smaller became the form that had been Benla'al. Lucifer could see the sight sickened his angels. His object lesson was having its desired effect. But he had to end it before he pushed them too far.

"You have punished him enough, my little ones. Come to your reward," Lucifer commanded. The black droplets left Benla'al and returned with eagerness to their master's mouth and body.

There were some among the angels who cried as they looked at their former friend. Others turned away in shame. Where a beautiful creature of light had once been, there now drifted a wasted, foul-smelling mass.

"*I . . . still serve . . . my God.*"

The strangled words coming from the formless mass surprised them all – especially Lucifer. Rage twisted his features. He made a giant fist and backhanded Benla'al with all his might. "Be gone from my presence forever!" he screamed.

The wounded, burned angel should have careened into the planet. Instead, he did something no one expected.

Benla'al disappeared in a blinding flash of light. Like Stavros, he had *unbecome*.

———

Rendall and Grisson slipped from the portal into the dark universe. They eased themselves toward the smaller body of matter floating near the planet, but discovered stealth was unnecessary. Far beneath them, close to the planet's surface, chaos reigned. As they hid themselves behind a rocky outcrop, Rendall pointed to a black mist scattering the angels left and right.

Grisson shuddered and gripped Rendall hard. "Who is the angel being attacked by that foul mist? I heard Lucifer and him arguing earlier."

"His name is Benla'al," Rendall explained. "In the past, he counted himself one of Lucifer's most loyal angels." They both watched as Lucifer recalled the mist into his mouth. Rendall wiped a hand across his face as if he could taste the black droplets. He grimaced and turned his head away. "It looks as if Benla'al refuses to follow his leader's new direction."

The angel known as a gifted teacher could remember everything he heard. Lucifer's confession of what he'd done and become by disobeying God riveted him. But his attention shifted when Grisson suddenly jumped up, trembling.

"What are you doing?" Rendall whispered. He grabbed the little angel around the middle and held on for dear life.

Grisson, for his part, struggled to escape. He pushed at his teacher's hands, trying to free his powerful wings and thrust himself upwards.

"Let me go!" he hissed. "We've got to help Benla'al escape."

Rendall, hair flying everywhere, refused to let go. "Calm down and listen to me," he insisted. Grisson still struggled. For a long moment, Rendall feared he couldn't hold him. "Please, for the sake of God and Heaven, sit down and listen."

Perhaps the mention of God finally got through to the little angel. He slumped to the ground. Disappointment clouded his face as he looked at Rendall. "What's the matter with you? We've got to help that poor angel."

Rendall wouldn't give in. "What we must do is obey Michael's orders. We are supposed to learn all we can and report back to him." He jabbed a finger in Grisson's chest for emphasis. "There's more at stake here than one angel. It's our responsibility to figure out what Lucifer is planning so Michael can stop him. Our getting caught while trying to be heroes won't help Benla'al or anyone else." He released Grisson but stayed close, ready to grab him again, if necessary.

His pupil looked at him hard, obviously thinking about what he'd said. Then, with a brief nod, he turned back to watch the action. "You're right. I'm sorry. It won't happen again."

But when Benla'al, burned and disfigured, proclaimed his allegiance to God, both angels had difficulty staying put. The sudden *unbecoming* that followed stunned them to silence.

Lucifer had clearly become something far more powerful than anyone could have ever imagined.

"The Well of Power." Rendall tried to get his thoughts stirring. "As long as he has access to the Well, he'll become more and more powerful." He inched his face close to Grisson's. Rendall wanted to remind the little angel of his first lesson in the cavern path. Like the truths imparted during that first light cycle, failure to learn this lesson could mean disaster for all the angels.

"Remember everything you see, everything you hear. You can't count on my being with you when you return to Heaven." Rendall's eyes drilled into Grisson.

"Don't talk like that." Grisson turned pale, the wan color of his face visible even in the darkness. "You're scaring me."

Rendall eased up a bit. He had to keep reminding himself this angel had been created but three light cycles ago. His learning curve, from the beginning, had been pretty steep.

"I'm planning on coming back with you, Grisson. There's lots more I want to learn about God and Heaven. But both of us have to be ready for any contingency."

As they shifted their attention to Lucifer, Grisson muttered, "I'll be ready, but we'd better go back together. I don't want to have to explain why you didn't come with me. That Stondrin asks too many questions."

Despite himself, Rendall grinned.

A shout from the Well's vicinity changed his expression. Events were getting out of hand, and nothing in his experience prepared him for what he saw.

CHAPTER FIFTEEN

"This is the answer!" Lucifer exulted. "I have the power to destroy anyone who opposes me!"

The angels in his command might be shocked by another of their own being *uncreated*, but Lucifer wasted no emotion on the small minded and unfaithful. Couldn't they see what lay within their grasp? Didn't they realize what a wonderful leader they served? –

Or did they truly serve him? He had to find out who would be loyal in the battle he knew might soon be coming.

"I am as God, now," Lucifer boasted. "I can create and uncreate." His eyes swept the troops assembled before him. "Those who do not wish to serve me had better leave now. I will not tolerate angels in my command who won't follow where I lead. I expect and demand complete loyalty."

Many of the angels turned to go, but a shout stopped them.

"Hold a moment!"

They turned to see Lucifer reach into the Well and withdraw pure power.

"Do any of you have a desire to become stronger? I can give you anything you wish: more power, greater beauty . . . ." He swung toward Volthra'an, who had been one of those preparing to leave. "I told you earlier, stay with me and I'll make you the fastest flyer in all of Heaven. Leave, and you'll be the same slow, clumsy flier you've always been."

The thin angel bumped into several others as he turned around and flew back toward Lucifer and the Well of Power. "You really have the ability to do that?" he asked.

"I have the power to do whatever I wish," Lucifer responded. "But if I give you this gift, I must have your promise of loyalty."

"I have always wanted to be a great flyer," Volthra'an breathed. "But to be the best of all the angels . . . ." He took a deep breath and made the decision that would forever change him. "I will follow you, Lucifer."

"And here is your reward, my loyal one." Lucifer flung the power straight at Volthra'an.

The creative essence thinned out as it neared the angel. Needle-shaped, it pierced his eyes, using his pupils as a doorway into the would-be flyer. Volthra'an gave a choked moan and began to change. His wings turned a mottled gray. Black streaks appeared on his body, dulling the former purity of his skin. His feet blurred into cloven hooves. Long, deadly talons grew from his fingers. Slits appeared where his eyes had been, and a malevolent darkness stared out at the world.

The size of the former angel, however, shocked everyone. He grew almost as big as Lucifer. His wings elongated until they stretched to the height of ten angels, and when Volthra'an unfolded them, their power bowled over those nearest.

"Lucifer has his first recruit." On the far side of the small rock, Rendall shook his head. Bitterness filled his mouth. "To make it worse, Volthra'an used to be loyal to Michael."

"How can we stop this madness?" Grisson asked. Neither angel looked at the other as they talked. The incident unfolding beside the Well of Power riveted them.

"I have an idea," Rendall said. "Remember how Stavros disappeared when he touched the Well?"

Grisson nodded. "How does that help us, though?"

"Lucifer may be too powerful for us, but his followers won't be. If we can throw them into the Well of Power, they'll *unbecome*. Get rid of enough of Lucifer's followers, and his power disappears along with them. Alone, he cannot stand against us."

Rendall pulled on Grisson's shoulder. "Come on, let's get back to Michael and tell him." They watched Volthra'an's wings unfold. Grisson had a sick look on his face. "I'm afraid we've waited too long."

Rendall was unsure what he meant. But an instant later, he saw Grisson's words prove themselves true.

The light in the Well of Power swirled and pulsed, as if displeased with the recent unfolding of events. Beside it, the universe's new master looked over his first creation.

"All in all, I'm pleased with the new you, Volthra'an." Lucifer said. "You look strong and . . . unique. For my first creation, I think I did well." He beckoned his follower closer. "Tell me, how does your new body feel?"

No hint of the once-present awkwardness remained. Instead, intense speed seemed ready to burst out at any moment. Volthra'an stretched, reveling in the strong body. He looked over one shoulder at his huge wings and his eyes widened at the sight.

"I want to test these new powers, my lord." The raspy voice sounded not at all like the Volthra'an everyone had known. But then, that angel no longer existed.

Lucifer noted the different reactions of the angels to the being he'd created. Many of them looked repulsed by the change to their former friend. Others, however, saw his size and strength, and gazed upon him with naked envy. Lucifer knew he could manipulate these to his side. As for the others . . . .

"You have my permission to fly, Volthra'an."

"Yesss!" hissed his first follower. With a prodigious leap, he disappeared. The speed of Volthra'an's flight caught everyone, even his creator, by surprise. One moment he stood before them. An instant later the formerly clumsy flyer appeared far away. One flex of his wings had served to put him on the other side of the small rock near the planet. As he descended onto its rough surface, however, he looked startled. Volthra'an let loose an inarticulate roar and made a stabbing, downward motion with his hands. One more flex of his wings, and he reappeared before the stunned assembly. Two figures struggled in his hands, trying vainly to escape.

"Well, well. What have we here?" Lucifer purred. "Rendall, Grisson, how nice of you to drop in."

CHAPTER SIXTEEN

The Well of Power pulsed, throwing out the only visible light. Beneath them, Rendall could see the planet slowly turning. Deep gouges had appeared in its once smooth surface since the last time he had seen it. The muddy brown color of the planet was changing to a deeper black. The planet seemed to shudder as it orbited a now dead sun.

Lucifer floated before them all, delighted with the way things had turned out. His new power caused events to unfold in a way different than even he'd anticipated. Who needed God's purpose? Lucifer would show God and everyone else that he, Lucifer had the ability and the strength to rule and to determine his own destiny. After all, he had The Well of Power . . . . Ah, power! How it sang to him! Ready to be used -- just like the creatures in front of him at that moment.

Rendall watched as Lucifer reached into the Well of Power and drew out a handful of pure light. Lucifer drew back his hand as if to throw, and Rendall shielded his own face as best he could. "No! I refuse it!" he cried out.

Lucifer cocked his head to one side, as if considering the angel's words. "But that's why you came here, isn't it?" His dark eyes pinned Rendall and Grisson as surely as the talons holding them. "What other reason could you have for being here? Surely you're not spying for Michael?"

Rendall looked at Grisson out of the corner of his eyes, never turning his face from Lucifer. The little angel trembled like a cherubim flying through the Mists of Light. Volthra'an had to squeeze his talons tighter to keep a grasp on him. Lucifer saw it, too. He put out a huge hand and squeezed Grisson around the neck.

"I asked you a question." A menacing tone filled his voice. "And I expect an answer."

"Come on, Lucifer." Rendall spoke quickly. "You know he's only been created a short while. He knows little about anything happening. I brought him with me for added speed if we needed to get away."

Lucifer let go of Grisson's neck and swung around toward Rendall. He leaned in close to his face. "All right, *teacher*," he sneered. "I ask you the same question. Why are you here?"

"You know me," Rendall said as casually as possible. "I always want to learn more about everything. There's so much in this universe I still don't understand -- and it intrigues me. So when we saw you working on Volthra'an, we stopped to watch. After all, this is something you don't see every light cycle."

"Does Michael know you're here?" Lucifer asked.

Please, Rendall thought, *don't let Grisson say a word.* "You might as well know that Michael is busy gathering angels to discover why the light went out of Heaven for awhile. He didn't need us to do that, so I decided to come here and add to my knowledge base." All that was true, as far as it went.

"The light went out in Heaven?" one of the other angels blurted. Lucifer silenced him with a glance.

"In other words, Heaven has its own problems right now?" Lucifer looked thoughtful. "This just might work. Michael and his angels take care of Heaven. I and my followers will recreate and rule this universe as I see fit."

The self-proclaimed lord of the universe heaved a mock sigh

as he turned to address the watching angels. "I only have one problem, then, don't I? What am I to do to with these two? After all, I can't very well let them go running back to Michael and tell him everything I'm doing." His face split into a cruel grin. "But I don't want to destroy them, either. After all, I am a generous, loving leader."

He turned back to Rendall. "I have a perfect solution." Rendall's heart sank. He knew what was coming. "You can stay here with us and teach any new creations I decide to bring into being. To prove your loyalty to me" – Lucifer raised the handful of power again – "all you need do is allow me to make you stronger."

"You don't need me, Lucifer," Rendall replied.

"Of course I do." Lucifer's anger returned as suddenly as it had left. He hated any challenge to his authority, however mild. Having power and wielding it was now his only god.

"You don't need a teacher because you can't create anything." Rendall remained firm, though all hope now seemed distant.

Lucifer's face twisted in rage and he grabbed Rendall's face and squeezed. "You lie!" He gestured toward Volthra'an. "As you can see, I've already begun to create." He let go of the angel, and Rendall rubbed his tender jaw.

"Angels don't lie," Rendall retorted. "You've already forgotten that in your haste to fall to new lows." If *unbecoming* awaited him, he might as well be blunt. Maybe his words would persuade some of those listening to rebel against their leader.

"You only changed what God has already created," Rendall continued. "No one but God can create something from nothing. And you're *definitely* not God!"

"Whatever I am, it's far more than you are, stupid little teacher!" Lucifer raised the handful of power once more. "The time for talking is done."

"What's going to happen to them, Lucifer?" The question came from one of the other angels.

"That's their choice," Lucifer replied. "Grisson will follow his mentor's example. So if Rendall chooses to *unbecome*, he'll have the added guilt of knowing he caused another's demise, as well."

While Lucifer talked, his attention on the questioner, Rendall looked at Grisson. The angel's eyes were fixed on his teacher. Rendall mouthed silently, *"Be ready to fly."* He gestured with his eyes toward the portal. A single tear slipped down Grisson's face, but he nodded.

"It's time, Rendall." Lucifer held up the power before the angel's eyes. It glistened and swirled. Its beauty beckoned seductively to all who looked upon it.

Rendall swallowed hard and forced his eyes away from the light. "Remember your first lesson, Grisson. Never forget what I taught you in the cavern." He refused to look at or talk to Lucifer. "Those who oppose God will ultimately lose. Stay true to Him."

Lucifer slapped his free hand over Rendall's mouth. "Now I'm going to teach the teacher a lesson," he said with menace. "Rendall, you tell Grisson to be true to God, but where is He? Where is your mighty Master?"

He raised his voice so that all the angels could hear. "God has fled Heaven and this universe. He knows when He's met His match. My power is your only hope now."

An evil grin spread across Lucifer's face. "Now for another surprise. Volthra'an, give me Grisson."

When he had the little angel firmly in hand, Lucifer turned to his first servant. "I have given you the ability to make angels *unbecome*. Your first duty will be to send the teacher out of existence."

Grisson struggled within Lucifer's grasp. Somehow he had to help Rendall. Growing tired of the antics, Lucifer backhanded him across the jaw. The blow stunned Grisson and he fell over the big angel's arms. "Weakling," Lucifer taunted.

"What am I supposed to do, master?" Volthra'an asked.

"Touch Rendall's face with your other hand," Lucifer instructed. "Get as close to the eyes as possible. As you touch him, let hate flood your heart and wish that he was gone forever. Visualize the word *unbecome* floating before your eyes; repeat it over and over in your mind."

Volthra'an's face twisted in concentration as he moved a huge taloned hand ever closer to his captive's face. Rendall never struggled. He still refused to look at Lucifer, ignoring his presence. Instead, his eyes locked onto the silver portal. Tantalizing because of its closeness, it remained unreachable. Rendall's eyes widened slightly as Volthra'an touched the skin above his eyes . . . and he *unbecame* in a flash of light.

"Marvelous!" Lucifer crowed. He let go of the stunned Grisson, allowing him to float in front of him, and clapped his hands in glee. "How many of you want this kind of power for yourselves?"

"I'm ready," a voice called out.

Lucifer turned to the speaker. As he did so, Grisson sprang to life. He jumped backwards, out of Lucifer's reach, and blurred his wings in flight. The little angel headed straight for the portal and Heaven.

"Volthra'an!" Lucifer yelled. "Get him!"

CHAPTER SEVENTEEN

Lyntos sighed once more. It didn't matter how loud he sighed. He could even gripe aloud about his lousy assignment. No one would silence him. That's because no one else happened to be around. Tall and broad-shouldered, Lyntos wore a perpetual smile on his face. No matter what happened, his good nature could always be counted on to see the best side of things -- until now. Bored, he stood up and moved around a bit. He'd been sitting on the ledge next to the Mists for quite awhile, now.

Why couldn't he be with the rest of the angels on the cavern floor, planning for battle, discussing strategy, honing fighting skills? He wanted action, not inertia. Instead, all alone, he watched the portal into the universe.

Lyntos sighed again. His good nature began to take hold once more, and his signature smile appeared. It might be a lousy assignment. It might be boring. But Michael, his leader, had ordered him to carry it out.

Important, he'd said. Come tell me immediately if anything happens, he'd said. What am I watching for, Lyntos had asked. Don't worry, Michael had responded darkly, you'll know when you see it.

Now, for what must have been the millionth time, he spread

his wings and glided toward the portal. Not too close, though. Michael had warned him to maintain a healthy distance for his own protection. As if anything important would ever happen while he watched.

"Michael!"

Lyntos jumped back as Grisson, the spindly new angel, burst through the portal.

"Tell Michael" –

He managed to make it only half-way into Heaven. A startled look appeared on his face and he slipped back into the universe, dragged by an unseen force.

Lyntos found himself alone again. But the boredom had *definitely* vanished. He wheeled about and rushed for the cavern and Michael.

"Thought you'd get away from me, didn't you."

The voice hissed in Grisson's ear, and he found himself in the huge grip of Volthra'an. The former angel had matched him wing stroke for wing stroke in his flight to the silver portal. He had a bigger body, and those wings meant he could probably fly faster than Grisson. But . . . the angel who had been Volthra'an no longer existed. The intelligence and organizing skills had disappeared, replaced instead by bigger muscles and strong wings. Maybe that lack of intelligence could be exploited.

The spindly angel took his two thumbs and thrust hard into his captor's eyes. With a scream, Volthra'an let go of him and tried to rub away the pain.

"You can't get away!" Lucifer's servant roared, tears clouding his vision. "I'm still blocking the portal into Heaven."

No answer, however, came from his opponent.

Volthra'an shook his head, trying to clear away the pain and tears. He turned around. Grisson had somehow disappeared.

"The black hole, you fool!" Lucifer shouted. "He's headed for the other portal!"

Volthra'an got a glimpse of silver disappearing into the black hole. He bared his teeth in a cruel grin, spread his wings and shot toward his prey at an alarming speed. "Don't worry," he rasped. "I'll get him. The victory is mine this day."

Grisson flew as never before. He dove into the black hole, ignoring the cloying darkness. When he emerged, the little angel turned sharply to the right. The first portal lay straight ahead, a great distance away. If he had guessed right, however, his only hope in reaching it lay in doing the unexpected.

Volthra'an burst out of the black hole moments later. He had made up the distance between them in an instant. Sure enough, the former angel forged straight ahead. Grisson would have been captured if he'd continued on his previous course. Instead, he took off toward a distant star well to the side of the portal.

Volthra'an turned with difficulty. Grisson zipped behind a star and then turned hard to the left. A sharp talon grazed his side as he changed direction, and he gasped in pain. Volthra'an had unbelievable speed! The little angel realized, with a sinking feeling, he'd probably never make it back to Heaven.

Giving up, however, could not be an option. *Unexpected*, he thought. *Do the unexpected.*

"Here I come!" he cried, and reversed direction.

Grisson flew straight at the winged monstrosity and dived downward at the last instant. Volthra'an went for the feint. He stabbed downward with his talons and tried to impale Grisson. The angel, however, reversed direction and flew right into Volthra'an's face. Again, his thumbs jabbed into the former angel's eyes. Already sore, this new invasion caused Volthra'an to convulse in pain.

"Your *unbecoming* will be excruciating!" he managed to choke out at his tormenter.

Grisson shot toward the portal with all his might. No turns now. No detours. Volthra'an wouldn't fall for the same trick again. He breathed a prayer to God, wherever He might be, and watched as the portal seemed to approach at a crawl. It loomed before him in space, close but perhaps unattainable.

Volthra'an forced himself to ignore the pain. Hate overrode

everything else. He followed Grisson's flight through watery eyes. His jet-black pupils contracted until they were nothing but pin points. With a snarl, the muscular flyer launched himself at the hated angel, and in the blink of an eye, came within a few wingspans of Grisson. Volthra'an raised his talons and aimed them at the body in front of him.

Lyntos and Stondrin hurried to catch up with Michael. The big angel had wasted no time when Lyntos flew into the cavern with his news. He'd simply gestured at Stondrin to follow, before rushing toward the ledge and the portal. A company of angels followed farther behind, but their sheer numbers clogged the passageway through the cavern and slowed them down.

"Why didn't Grisson continue on into Heaven?" Michael called back over his shoulder.

"I don't know," Lyntos panted. "I think someone pulled him back before he could get completely through."

Stondrin pulled even with his leader. "Michael, that just doesn't make sense. There's no way anyone else in all of Heaven could come close to keeping up with Grisson when he flies."

"You're forgetting he's not in Heaven anymore. Who knows what Lucifer has come up with in that dark universe." Michael never stopped or slowed down as he spoke. His close-cropped hair lay flat against his head, as if willing the angel to further speed.

They soon left the passageway and surrounded the *Place of First Becoming*. Each one focused his attention on the silver doorway hanging in the Mists before them.

"What do we do now?" asked Lyntos. "Should we go after him?"

"We can't risk going out there." Michael's fists closed in frustration. "We don't know what we're facing. They could be anywhere, waiting to ambush us." He didn't like it, but they could do nothing except wait.

"Michael," Stondrin said, "Why don't we surround the portal? If Grisson tries to come through again, we can help him."

A flurry of sound, and the company of angels spilled onto and over the ledge. They hovered in the Mists and waited for instructions.

Michael raised his voice. "Stondrin has suggested we encircle the portal. Let's do it."

The angels gathered around the silver doorway. Under Michael's instructions, they positioned themselves wing to wing. Once in place, the beings of light formed an unbroken ring of protection.

"If you see Grisson begin to enter Heaven, grab him and pull him in," he ordered, looking around the circle. "We might have only a moment. So be prepared to act."

In the blackness of space, Grisson could sense an even deeper blackness rushing upon him. He strained for the nearby portal with all his might. Just as it seemed as if he'd make it, Grisson felt a shaft of pain lance through his back. Nausea shook him. He looked down to see one of Volthra'an's sharp talons sticking out of his chest. The force of the blow carried him through the surface of the portal. Silver swam before his eyes. Then Heaven's newest angel knew no more.

Volthra'an exulted in his speed and flying ability. *Lucifer granted my deepest desire*, he thought. The body he now inhabited wasn't elegant, but his strength more than made up for any other loss. Close behind the fleeing angel, Volthra'an made a fist with one long talon extended. He thrust forward with all his might and pierced Grisson completely through, from back to front.

He hadn't counted on the force of the blow carrying both of them into Heaven. For a moment, the prospect scared him. But then Volthra'an imagined the looks on the faces of his former friends as they saw him in his new form. How impressed they'd be! And maybe a little afraid of his strength and speed. The shock and fear should give him a few moments to do some real damage among the ranks of angels.

"I'll be Lucifer's favorite if I can stop Michael and *uncreate* several of his captains," he crowed. A strong flex of his wings would carry him out of harm's way and back through the portal if he got into trouble. His face twisted into a cruel grin. Michael and the others were going to be surprised!

"Grisson!" Stondrin shouted.

The little angel appeared suddenly in the portal. Most of the angels jumped back in surprise when they saw his condition. Grisson's head lolled, eyes closed. A gush of thick, silver liquid erupted from his mouth. And a sharp . . . something . . . had impaled his body.

Michael remained in place in spite of what he saw. Instead of jumping back like the others, he reached out to pull Grisson through the portal. He also tried to pull the little angel off of the sharp projection piercing him from back to front.

That's when Volthra'an made his surprise entrance into Heaven.

"Everybody get back!" Michael roared. He took the wounded angel and flew to where Stondrin had retreated. Thrusting Grisson into the curious angel's arms, he turned to see if everyone had obeyed him.

His instructions were unneeded. When the huge monstrosity called Volthra'an burst through the portal, the shocked onlookers were unprepared for what they faced. The intruder, three times as big as any of them, had a wingspan that dwarfed even the largest. His bulging strength overwhelmed the angels, and they leaped back in alarm.

"I've got to handle this," Michael shouted. "I'll fight him by myself."

How can anyone defeat this creature, thought Stondrin. *Michael is going to get himself impaled in the same way as Grisson, and then where will we be?* The biggest angel, now, in all of Heaven looked impossibly small as he engaged the invader. He drew back a fist and . . . .

"Unhh . . . Ssstop the pain . . . Can't bear the light!" Volthra'an twisted about in the air. He moaned and screamed, his enemies forgotten. Volthra'an threw up both arms to cover his face from the hated light.

As the angels watched, holes began appearing in the former angel. Each one produced a scream. He shuddered and grew pale. The screams thinned out to a soft wail. The holes widened until they joined together, leaving less and less of Lucifer's re-creation.

Then Volthra'an *was* no more.

The light of Heaven had destroyed the darkness.

CHAPTER EIGHTEEN

Power flew everywhere.

Lucifer drew from the Well of Power as fast as he could, flinging the creative essence with abandon. For their part, his followers chased the power down and allowed it to splash on them. Transformations occurred with alarming frequency. Muscles bulged, creatures grew in size, features twisted, sometimes tails formed. Snarls filled the air. Earthquakes tore the planet beneath them asunder, and a dark, lava-like substance seeped from the interior and spread across the surface.

Some of the angels refused to participate in the reshaping. They huddled apart from the newly-changed creatures, unsure of what the future held for them. Dalsa'in spoke in a soft whisper to the group. "Be patient. There may be a moment when we can break for the portal and escape this lunacy."

"What happens if they notice us before then?" The quavering voice could have belonged to any of them.

Dalsa'in continued to speak softly. He tried to calm himself, as well as the others. "If we have to *unbecome* in order to stay true to our God, then so be it." He held up a hand to forestall any more outbursts. "Just like you, I'm not in a hurry to undergo anything I don't have to. But if we try to force this too soon, we may all find ourselves no longer a part of Heaven or this universe."

The angels hoped God would intervene with some miracle that could deliver them. In the presence of Lucifer's imposing figure, however, the price of hope climbed even as its certainty diminished. The self-proclaimed lord of the universe still grew and changed. From time to time, he would pause in his efforts to build a personal army and swallow another handful of power. His beauty became only greater, his voice even more seductive. A low hum of power surrounded him as he worked. Greater and greater handfuls of creative essence flew ever farther and faster. The creatures grew stronger and more horrible.

Dalsa'in swallowed hard. He saw no way out.

———

"Is he going to be okay, Michael?"

Stondrin willingly gave up his burden to the big angel. Michael held Grisson tenderly, as if he were the most precious creation in all the Eternal Country. Come to think of it, Stondrin realized, maybe he was.

Grisson looked horrible. Already thin, the terrible wound in his chest and back served to make him seem even smaller. The thick flow of silver from his mouth had slowed, but another had begun in his chest when the cruel talon was removed. Grisson's eyes fluttered and his body jerked spasmodically.

"Look at his eyes," someone whispered.

The pupils became paler as the silver substance bled out of him. The fluttering began to slow; the jerking grew weaker. "He will *unbecome* soon if something isn't done," LeSage stated. "I've got an idea. Follow me." Michael wheeled around and flew for the cavern. Stondrin had never seen him move so fast. The others trooped behind as best they could. Worried glances between many of them were not lost on Stondrin. Like him, they feared for Grisson's existence.

The River of Light twisted and turned on the cavern floor like something alive. No one could ever be sure what course it would take through the immense training ground of the angels. The good thing about this portion of the River was its depth. In some places, you could lie down without it covering your face.

Michael reached the drop-off point of the cavern and never paused. He dove over the side and streaked toward the River of Light far below. Concern for his friend drove him. Grisson might be new; he might be small; he definitely worried too much about hurting everyone's feelings. But the courage he had shown in the face of incredible danger was enormous. Michael had to save him, if possible.

A surprise awaited him when he reached the cavern floor. The River, playful and unpredictable as long as anyone could remember, began to pool. It formed a uniform depth just right for Grisson. Michael laid his friend in the River, face up. Stondrin and LeSage flew down and landed on either side of the little angel. The three of them watched the liquid light flow over and around him. As other angels entered the cavern, they encircled the pool, becoming a celestial barricade to keep anyone from disturbing Grisson's fight to remain *created*.

Quiet pervaded the cavern. The only sound came from the light as it bathed the angel in its midst. Other angels who fell into the River of Light always glowed immediately. Grisson, however, lay unchanged. Michael glanced at Stondrin and gave a small shake of his head. It wasn't working. They may have been too late.

"Michael, who or what was the creature that did this to Grisson?" asked Stondrin

Michael took his eyes off Grisson for a moment to respond. "I have no idea. I've never seen anything like it before." His voice sounded tired. Hair lay wet and limp across his forehead, and he rubbed his eyes in frustration.

"Look!" LeSage whispered.

A small whirlpool had formed in the midst of the light.

Directly over the terrible wound, it sucked the River of Light down and into Grisson. The paleness receded and a healthy glow began to appear around his upper body.

"Scoop up some of the light and pour it on his face," Michael commanded.

The three angels used their hands to gently splash the light onto their friend. Wherever the River touched Grisson now, he began to glow. His eyes fluttered open. Everyone could see the brightness in them grow, as if he were a vessel being filled with divine fuel. The wound grew smaller and finally closed with a hiss.

The little angel raised his head and looked around. "How did I get here?" he asked.

CHAPTER NINETEEN

"Form up!"

Michael's words galvanized the angels. At last, here was an order easy to obey! Companies found their places on the cavern floor. Over a hundred thousand angels spread out in orderly fashion. Captains stood at the front of each group, ready to lead.

Grisson's friends helped him to his feet as angels solemnly moved here and there, finding their proper place. Still a bit weak, he trailed his hand in the River of Light, and then sat down abruptly.

"Let me stay here a moment longer," he said.

Michael patted him softly on the shoulder. "You can sit there as long as you like. What you've done for Heaven today is incredible."

"I've done nothing more than Stavros or Benla'al or . . . or Rendall." As he spoke Rendall's name, tears formed in his eyes.

"I'd thought Rendall must have paid the ultimate sacrifice. You never would have returned without him." Michael motioned to Stondrin and LeSage. The three knelt in the shallow pool of light beside Grisson.

The little angel struggled to pull himself together; God's

cause demanded his best. He stood up, using Michael for support. "I need to report," he whispered in Michael's ear. "Is this information for you alone, or do you want everyone to hear?"

"Everyone deserves to hear this," Michael said. "The others will be just as involved as we are."

The leader of Heaven's angels called for silence. "I want everyone here to know even more terrible times are facing us." That got everyone's attention! "There may be a battle. To better understand what we all will be facing, I've asked Grisson to tell us what he and Rendall saw during their time away from Heaven."

He turned to Grisson. "Go ahead. I want as much detail as possible."

Grisson took a deep breath and began. He described everything he'd seen, from the moment the two angel spies had arrived in the universe, hiding behind the small rock. The re-creation of Volthra'an, their discovery by him, the insights of Rendall concerning how to defeat Lucifer and his followers -- he left nothing out. Grisson didn't falter until he began telling of Rendall's *unbecoming*.

"Above all, he remained faithful to our God," Grisson said, weeping now. Nor was he the only one. Tears flowed down the cheeks of many of those assembled. Rendall had been greatly loved and revered.

"How did you get back here?" Stondrin asked.

Grisson explained about how he'd escaped to the second portal, only to be dragged back by Volthra'an. When he got to the part about jabbing his thumbs in his pursuer's eyes, several of the angels showed grim smiles and nodded their approval.

"As we approached the first portal, something happened to my back," Grisson said. "I don't remember anything else until I woke up here on the cavern floor. But I'm guessing Volthra'an stabbed me with one of his talons." He looked to Michael for confirmation.

"That monstrosity that came into Heaven was Volthra'an?" Michael asked in a shocked voice.

Grisson nodded. "There is a terrible price to be paid for deserting God and following Lucifer.

"By the way," he added. "Whatever happened to Volthra'an?"

"The light of Heaven punched holes in the creature of darkness until he was no more," answered LeSage.

"That's as good a way of putting it as anyone could have done," Stondrin said.

Michael spread his wings and ascended until all could see him. "We know our enemy: Lucifer and his minions," he called out. "We know our purpose: defend Heaven and destroy evil. It's time to go to battle!"

The vast chamber floor rang out with the cheers of angels.

The huge, lithe figure moved with grace and speed in the shadows of the new universe. Touching, reshaping, each creature received Lucifer's personal attention. When he had finished designing his followers, they gathered in front of him. Dalsa'in noticed the former angels shying away from the Well of Power. They shrank into the darkness as much as possible, as if even that little bit of light harmed them.

Lucifer waited until he had everyone's attention. Then he spoke. "This is a glorious moment for all of us. At last we are masters of our own destiny. Nothing can hold us back now!"

A cacophony of sound rose up from the creatures listening to their leader. Snarling, grunting, roaring, they showed their approval of what Lucifer said. Several fights broke out in the back of the ranks, as some wanted to test their new strength on someone perceived weaker. Onlookers who tried to break up a scuffle found themselves drawn into the fray. Fists flew, bites were exchanged, fangs bared.

Lucifer couldn't believe it. Anarchy threatened to tear apart his brand new army. Several creatures bumped into him as they fought. He picked up each in one hand and threw them into the middle of the battle, scattering creatures everywhere.

"Enough!" he screamed. "The next one to continue fighting will be *uncreated*."

Several of his followers refused to stop. Their hatred for each other made them oblivious to everything else. One of them, bigger than the rest, readily showed his disdain of Lucifer's power by continuing to fight. Horns jutted from his head and a huge, powerful tail cowed anyone foolish enough to come near. He bent his hapless opponent backwards over his knee and a loud "pop" reverberated throughout the immediate area. The other creature screamed once and went limp. The victor shouted , "I'm the strongest!" and raised his arms in elation – but only for a moment. In the corner of his vision, a terrible darkness swept toward him, and the creature known as Lestras turned to face his doom.

Lucifer flew to within inches of his face. "Let me show you what my touch can do." He spoke to everyone, though his eyes never left the strong creature in front of him. The next words came in a soft, menace-filled tone. "You have disobeyed me, Lestras. Do you know what that means?"

Lestras bowed his head. "I beg your forgiveness, master," he said.

"There can be no forgiveness," came the response.

Lestras raised his head and looked at Lucifer with slitted eyes. "Then perhaps, *Master,* it's time you learned a lesson, as well." And in that same instant, he whipped his powerful tail in an arc at Lucifer's face. The speed was astonishing. In those close quarters, Lucifer had no time to dodge the terrible blow.

Instead, he opened his mouth.

The tail smashed into Lucifer's teeth, and the watching creatures waited for him to fall back, maimed and weakened. When the blow landed, however, Lucifer remained unmoved. No broken teeth or bruised mouth could be seen. He floated before Lestras, holding the creature's tail between his teeth.

Then Lucifer closed his mouth on the tail and began to chew.

Before their horrified eyes, his followers watched Lucifer consume Lestras. Alive until the end, the former angel at first beat at his master with all the considerable muscle and strength he had. It mattered not at all. The blows were as ineffectual as if Lucifer's opponent had been a baby. At the end, Lestras wept.

"Master," he pleaded. "I'll never disobey you again. Please forgive me."

The powerful teeth moved ever upward, never stopping. Lucifer crushed his chest and Lestras screamed. "At least stop the pain. It's unbearable," he groaned. His pleas finally changed to an incoherent babble, until Lucifer's teeth engulfed him completely.

A loud "snap" sounded. Lucifer's teeth closed on nothing. Lestras was but a memory. Lucifer looked around, as if still hungry for something -- or someone -- to eat. The other creatures backed away. No one wanted to follow where Lestras had gone.

"Remember this: there is no forgiveness with me," Lucifer proclaimed. He looked around at his stunned followers. "Forgiveness is for God, and God is a weakling who speaks of love and compassion."

The fallen angel patted his stomach with satisfaction. "I'm stronger than anyone in Heaven or this universe. If you don't like it, that's too bad. Now that I've re-created you there's no turning back."

He turned to the limp, broken victim of Lestras. "I promised to show you what I can do with my touch." He reached for the creature, only to see him try to pull away.

"Don't worry, I won't hurt you." He caressed the former angel's back. Wherever his fingers touched, a black stain appeared for a moment, then seeped into the skin. The anguish left the wounded one's face and his eyes regained their dark intensity. The spine straightened out, and a few moments later, the creature spread his wings and flew back and forth in front of the assembly, completely well.

"Thank you, Lucifer!" he said in a worshipful tone. "You have my total allegiance." A chorus of assent echoed his words. More than anything else, every creature wanted to prove his loyalty to Lucifer at that moment.

"What can I do to repay your generosity?" the healed creature asked.

"When the time comes," Lucifer said to them all, "destroy as many angels as possible and you'll have my praise and gratitude."

Lucifer allowed himself to sink to the planet's surface. The others followed, and he motioned for them to sit down and listen. "I am not without compassion," he lied. "I can heal you *if I wish it*. But I can also punish those who will not obey."

Many listening shuddered at the last remark. The crunching sounds of Lucifer's sharp teeth still reverberated in their ears.

Good, Lucifer thought. *Let them learn from Lestras*. He cared not a whit for the other creature he healed. But they didn't have to know that. Quite simply, he needed to have as many warriors as possible for the coming battle.

"Now it's time for you to learn more about your new powers."

Lucifer turned toward the group of angels huddled on the far side of the Well of Power. "Did you think I'd forgotten about you?" With a feral smile, he said, "I'm planning to use you to educate my army."

The healed creature still lurked beside Lucifer. "Take some others," his master said to him, "and bring the angels to me." They leaped to do his bidding.

Thank you, God, Dalsa'in thought. *Now I understand your words. Help me to be faithful to the end.* But he wondered if God could still hear him.

"Where will we come out when we go through the portal, Michael?" The archangel was glad to see LeSage thinking and participating again.

"Good question, LeSage" he responded. "I've got a theory, but we won't know if it works until we try it. So, we'll have to be ready for anything when we exit the portal into the universe."

The angels surrounded the silver portal. Never had they looked more beautiful or powerful. Their coming task seemed to infuse them with a holy strength. Ranks and companies reflected light on and around the cliffs as the Mists bathed them with a celestial brilliance. Michael regarded them with great affection. None had asked to be left in Heaven. Not one angel had expressed a desire to stay out of the action.

"What's your theory?" Stondrin asked, his eyebrows rising as he spoke. Naturally, it would be Stondrin. Michael smiled for what might be the last time in a great while.

"I believe we can determine our own place of exit," he explained. "If we *will* ourselves to come out by the black hole, we just might succeed in doing it. Concentrate on coming out by the planet instead, and that area will probably be what we'll see upon exiting."

He ran a hand through his hair. "Am I sure this will work? No. But I have to believe God knew these events would occur. This might well be one of the ways He has decided to help us."

"Where is God?" someone asked.

"Yes, why isn't He helping us?" Another voice sounded almost defiant.

"Could it be that Lucifer is right? Is he now stronger than God?" Shi'intor broke rank and flew toward Michael. "Has God run away because He's afraid?" he demanded. "Has He left us here to fight a battle He is unwilling to face Himself?"

"Get back in formation, Shi'intor," Michael ordered. "I'll answer every question as best I can. But I won't have chaos among my troops." When Shi'intor continued to advance on Michael, his captain flew up behind him and grabbed a wing. With a squawk, the angel found himself stopped in his tracks and hauled back into place.

"Thank you, Shi'intor, for obeying my orders so promptly." Several of the angels chuckled under their breath, but no one said anything.

"To answer your question: I don't know where God is. LeSage says He has left Heaven and gone away."

"What are we going to do?" someone wailed.

Michael glared at everyone. "Don't panic. Instead, remember God's love for you. Remember what it felt like in His throne room to be immersed in His love and to look upon His presence." He stared Shi'intor down. "Do you think Someone who loves us that much will desert us because of cowardice?"

Michael could see the angels starting to relax. "I believe that Lucifer's rebellion right at the start of a New Age is not a coincidence. Through all of this, my theory is that God has a plan, and we are a part of it with what we're doing right now."

"*My* theory. *I* believe." Shi'intor's words dripped with derision. "You could also be wrong and leading us to our destruction."

A shocked silence followed this pronouncement. Had Michael misjudged his angels? Were they unwilling to follow his leadership? Did they not want to follow God, no matter what the outcome?

"I believe him," Stondrin spoke into the silence.

"I also believe Michael." LeSage, bless him, continued getting stronger and stronger!

One by one, the others voiced their approval, and Shi'intor's rebellion dwindled away. The dissident angel flew quietly in place, silent now, but with a stubborn look of displeasure on his face. Michael knew that one could cause trouble.

A deep rumble shook the area where Lucifer and his army camped. The planet was becoming more unstable every moment. Nearby, a volcano spouted flames and molten rock. Thick lava burned its way down the slopes. A sulfurous stench filled the air.

Boulders flew at the group but passed through them. Lucifer didn't understand it. Somehow, they were in the universe; but at the same time, they weren't. Given enough time, however, he'd find a way to create a portal like God had done. Then, the universe would truly be his.

He let no one see his doubts, but Lucifer wondered what the future held for him. God's disappearing bothered him. How could he fight an opponent who wasn't there? The Well of Power also nagged at his thoughts. God had created many angels and, he assumed, most of Heaven without the Well. Why begin using it now? Could it be a trap?

He shook his head, frustrated. The fallen angel couldn't afford to think like that now. God must have made a mistake in judgment. The Creator would never knowingly have created something that would allow his angels to be destroyed. If God had made a mistake, that meant He was not omniscient, as He claimed. And if He had made a mistake in one area, He could very well make mistakes of judgment in other areas.

Lucifer smiled as he thought about defeating God. He would not doubt his own abilities again. Watching the planet careen ever more wildly in its path about the now-dead sun, he realized this place would never be home to Mankind. He was on the verge of winning everything!

"We'll never bow to you, Lucifer!"

He sighed and turned from the beauty of a planet destroying itself. Some unpleasant work still remained.

CHAPTER TWENTY

"Grisson, tell us the idea you and Rendall came up with to defeat Lucifer and his followers."

The little angel looked at Michael in astonishment. Grisson's silver complexion began to show a slight reddish color as a flush stole across his face. "Umm, couldn't you tell them instead?" he whispered.

Michael shook his head. "Sorry, Grisson. You know more about this than anyone else. I need you to give the other angels the necessary information and be available to answer any questions they have."

"Okay," Grisson sighed. "I'll do my best."

He put his back to the portal, raised his voice and addressed his fellow angels. "This idea really came from Rendall. He gave his life to ensure we would have the key to defeating Lucifer's forces." He paused and cleared his throat. "The creatures cannot *uncreate* you unless they touch you on or around your eyes. That seems to be the focal point of the creative essence within us. If we can grab them from behind and immobilize their hands and arms, we just might be able to carry them to the Well of Power and throw them in. Once they touch its interior, they'll *unbecome*. If we do this to enough of Lucifer's forces, he'll be vulnerable.

His power is great, but our numbers can overwhelm him if we're careful."

Grisson looked at Michael for confirmation before going on to the next step in the plan. The archangel nodded for him to continue.

"Rendall suggested, and Michael agrees, that we should work in teams of at least two. In that way, we'll be able to watch each other's back. Also, it'll take two to carry a creature to the Well of Power."

"Form into teams of two or three now," Michael ordered.

The angels began choosing partners for the coming battle. Michael noted with approval that a good deal of talking about fighting styles, and comparing strengths and weaknesses went on between them. Each angel wanted to be part of a strong team that had members able to work smoothly with one another. When the teams had formed, however, Telsha'in and Grisson remained unchosen.

"What are you going to do with these last two angels?" someone asked from the group. "Neither one is good for fighting."

Both angels ducked their heads at the words. Grisson noticed, however, that an amused smile played across Michael's face. "Telsha'in is Heaven's choirmaster. He will sing as we go into battle. I know these fallen angels cannot stand the light of Heaven. It may well be the music of our God, sung by Heaven's best, will be a weapon to distract and weaken them." Telsha'in pulled his shoulders back and cleared his throat, as if ready to fulfill his part in battle.

"As for Grisson . . . ." Michael turned to look at the little angel. "He will be my partner. I've not found a better fighter in all of the Eternal Country."

A snort of disbelief followed these words. "Come on, Michael, don't handicap yourself like that. Grisson might be fast in flight, but he doesn't look as if he could knock over a cherubim! You're crucial to our success."

Fradyn, who considered himself the most gifted of fighters after Lucifer and Michael, flew boldly up to Grisson. His massive bulk dwarfed the little angel. "Why don't you team up with someone like me and leave Grisson here to guard Heaven." He smiled as he said it, but the words still stung.

Grisson bit his lip. He didn't want to hurt anybody's chances in the coming conflict. Maybe he should back off and let the others do the fighting. After all, he knew himself to be a thin, spindly nothing.

To his amazement, however, Michael grinned bigger than ever.

"It's time for all of you to learn a lesson," Michael said. "Don't ever think I do anything other than what is best for my God. Fradyn, choose one of your teammates to help you with a task."

The big angel looked puzzled for a moment. Then he called out, "Toldin, come here."

A sleek, well-muscled angel glided from the group. His hair sat atop his head in tight curls, mimicking the tightly wound reflexes everyone knew could explode during an encounter with an opponent. Those reflexes had made Toldin one of the best fighters of all the angels. Coming to Fradyn's side, the two looked formidable.

"What are we supposed to do?" Toldin asked.

"The two of you are to catch Grisson and rub his face into the side of this cliff. In order to keep him from flying away from you, I'm giving Grisson the same order."

Michael directed his next words to the little angel. "I know you don't like to hurt others. So be gentle with them, but rub their faces in the side of the cliff."

Fradyn stared at Michael. "You've got to be kidding! This is a farce and a waste of time. Grisson doesn't have a chance against us. He couldn't defeat either one of us with our wings tied behind our backs, much less the two of *us* together. Toldin and I have spent untold light cycles on the cavern floor perfecting our fighting skills."

Michael's eyes grew cold. "I gave you an order, Fradyn. You might think it foolish, but you'll still obey my orders." Fradyn, to his credit, nodded his head and turned to face Grisson.

"Begin," Michael said.

Toldin dove for Grisson's middle. In a long-practiced move of teamwork, Fradyn moved behind and above the two to cut off those avenues of escape. Grisson, faced with no other alternative, folded his wings and let himself fall away from his attackers. Both Toldin and Fradyn had anticipated this, however. They sped downwards and angled toward each other like pincers closing on their foe. That's when Grisson did the unexpected. In a move that left everyone gasping, he unfolded his wings, blurred them impossibly fast, and shot straight upward. Fradyn's head snapped back as Grisson clipped his chin on the way up. Once above him, Grisson sped around to the stunned angel's wings and grabbed them. Fradyn now had no means of flight. He found himself falling like a rock and powerless to control where the two of them were going. Again, Grisson blurred his wings again and they passed Toldin as if he were standing still. The little angel angled his opponent toward the cliffs. At the last moment, he slowed his flight and let go of the angel. Fradyn slammed into the cliff, but at a much slower speed, thanks to Grisson's divine brakes. Everyone watching knew Grisson could have hurt him much worse, had he wished to.

"You're out of the fight, Fradyn," Michael said. "Toldin, he's all yours – if you can handle him."

Wary now, Toldin approached Grisson, who suddenly didn't look quite so small and harmless.

"I'm sorry about Fradyn," Grisson apologized. "And, I want you to know what's coming so you won't get hurt."

"Save your concern," Toldin shot back. "You surprised us the first time. Now it's different. I've fought hundreds of matches and lost very few of them. Get ready to defend yourself!"

Grisson continued as if he hadn't heard a word Toldin said. "I'm going to feint several times. But when you feel me grab your left foot, prepare to cover your face. That's when I'll be getting ready to swing you into the cliff wall. With your hands already up, your face will be protected." Then he swung a leg straight into Toldin's middle. The other angel never moved. At the last moment, Grisson stopped the kick and went for Toldin's foot.

"Gotcha!" Toldin hadn't fallen for the feint. He pulled his feet back and lunged for the back of Grisson's exposed neck. His famous reflexes had served him well. The little angel moved even faster than Toldin, however. He continued down and to the right. Toldin followed him in a steep dive, but -- surprise! -- Grisson wasn't there.

The angel felt a sharp tug on his left foot. Grisson had flown so fast he'd somehow gotten above and behind Toldin. Because he'd been turning to the right, Toldin knew Grisson would use his momentum to swing him even faster. He remembered the little angel's instructions and raised his hands. His fingers grazed the cliff wall. But at the last possible moment, Grisson pulled him in the other direction, slowing his speed and keeping him from injury.

Just like Michael had instructed.

Wild applause sounded from the watching angels. As usual, Grisson seemed embarrassed at all the attention.

"Sorry to have to do that," Michael said, not sounding sorry at all. "If I hadn't, though, most of you wouldn't have believed what I'm getting ready to tell you: Grisson has been my choice of partner since before Lucifer fell from Heaven."

He looked at the two whipped angels. "Do you believe me now?"

They nodded a weary yes. "Grisson, you may be the best I've ever faced," Fradyn admitted. "You have my admiration and respect." To the little angel's astonishment, Fradyn even grinned as he added, "I'll try not to let appearances deceive me ever again."

The Mists of rainbow-colored light bathed both victor and vanquished in a healing balm. Several of the other angels joined the three in the Mists. They raised their face toward scintillating light and drank in the pure brilliance of Heaven. Even Michael allowed himself a few moments of rejuvenation. He knew the looming battle would test every bit of his strength and courage.

After a time, Michael turned reluctantly from The River of Light. The time had come to reenter the darkness of the universe. But first, another lesson remained for Toldin, Fradyn and the others to learn. "Everyone back in formation," he called out.

Once his forces had returned to their places, Michael motioned Grisson and Telsha'in to his side. "Now for a confession," he said. "Lucifer and I fought against Grisson. He bested both of us."

"Wait a moment," Grisson protested. "I didn't beat you together. I fought only one at a time!"

The angels exploded in laughter. A puzzled Grisson turned to Michael for an explanation. "Why is that so funny?"

"Let me try to answer him," Toldin said. He gestured toward the thousands of watching angels. "None of the other angels in Heaven has *ever* beaten either Michael or Lucifer. We've not even come close. To think you have to explain that you *only* beat them one at a time says more to me than even fighting you did." He shook his head in amusement. "I think you're far better than you realize."

"I'm just lucky, that's all. I caught all of you by surprise."

A chorus of laughs exploded once again and Grisson turned red. "Maybe you ought not to say anything else about your fighting ability," Michael suggested.

He's as amused as the others, Grisson thought sourly. They didn't understand he had no idea what he was doing when he fought. He just followed instinct.

But he decided to keep that thought to himself.

"Dalsa'in," Lucifer said to the formerly quiet, ordinary angel before him, "Whether or not you care to serve under my authority is insignificant to me. However, if you're too dense to see that my way is best, then you're not worthy of existence."

He motioned to his creatures for attention. "Your powers are great, but they are still untested. I don't want you going into battle ignorant of the weapons at your disposal. I believe Michael won't be able to leave well enough alone. He and the other angels may soon be invading this universe, trying to stop us from expanding our base of power." He looked toward the distant slice of silver that led into what he feared was now forbidden territory. "Volthra'an, in spite of his powers, didn't return from Heaven. I must assume he's been destroyed. And I think I know why."

Lucifer gestured to the horns, cloven feet, and other obvious changes in his followers. "As you can see, you're not the same. I have transformed you from the weaklings you used to be into creatures of great size and strength. But, with your new strength, there has also come the ability to be comfortable in the darkness. That means Heaven is off-limits to any of you. Its light might destroy you. I believe that's what happened to Volthra'an. His strength and speed were such that no angel otherwise could have overcome him."

"Where will we live, master?" one of the creatures asked.

"Don't worry about that. We have this entire, wonderfully dark universe at our disposal. I'm going to recreate it to suit our new natures. And each time I eat from the Well of Power, I learn even more about how to manipulate matter. The best is yet to come for all those who remain loyal to me."

The cheers and snarls began again as the foul, evil creatures pledged themselves anew to Lucifer. He noticed, however, that his speech had fallen on deaf ears with the small band of "uncooperative" angels. The time had come to eliminate them. And he would teach both angels and creatures a lesson while doing so.

"I'm sure Volthra'an destroyed Grisson before he could get back to Heaven," Lucifer explained. "There's no way that scrawny brat could out-fly my magnificent creation. And that means you have a weapon the angels are unaware of. But"-- he held up a warning hand to forestall their cheering -- "it takes some effort to discover how to use it. So it's time to learn how to make someone *unbecome*. These angels will be your practice targets." He gave the prisoners a dismissive glance. "They're not much good for anything else."

Lucifer divided the creatures into groups and had them encircle an angel. "There aren't enough angels to go around," he explained. "Each group will take one angel. Touch his eyes or forehead, think about him *unbecoming*, and will him away. Don't worry if you can't get it right the first time." A cruel smile exposed his infamous teeth to the angels. "Practice makes perfect."

The creatures leaped with alacrity to obey their leader. At last, a chance to do something to please their master!

"Fly in all directions!" Dalsa'in shouted to the little band. A hopeless situation faced them, but they had to try. He watched as angels sprang up without hesitation. Some flew toward the Well of Power. Others tried for the portal. One of them, more imaginative than the rest, surprised everyone by heading straight into the volcano.

A huge hand clamped down on Dalsa'in's neck, effectively stopping him from going anywhere. Lucifer's voice sounded in his ear. "Good try, but it won't work. Watch what happens."

The creatures might still be learning about their powers, but their reflexes and speed were already remarkable. None of those trying to escape made it more than a few yards before one or more of Lucifer's followers pounced on them. Even the volcano proved no help. The angel fleeing toward it found himself being hauled down from behind by a gray and black scaled creature of incredible strength. It reached out and grabbed the would-be fugitive's leg, giving it a casual twist. A cry of pain ripped through the air, and those watching could see the leg broken at the knee. It stood out perpendicular to the rest of the body. The angel allowed himself to be dragged back to the group, moaning softly and trying to keep weight off the leg.

"I'm nothing if not compassionate," Lucifer said to the one with the shattered leg. "I can tell you are in pain. I assure you that I'll do everything in my power to make sure your pain disappears in just a few moment . . . along with you." He roared at his own joke and motioned to his followers to continue with their learning.

The angels still struggled with their captors, but the creatures outnumbered them. The fallen angels followed their leader's instructions. They broke into groups, each with an angel, and began their evil machinations. Lucifer chose to spare Dalsa'in, at least for the moment. He still hoped to turn the angel and make Dalsa'in a powerful leader of his troops. Horror enveloped his captive's face as Dalsa'in watched friends and fellow angels writhe about, scream and then vanish forever.

Nausea rose in Dalsa'in's throat as Lucifer's followers grew more excited. The carnage and destruction only made the creatures stronger. They pushed one another aside to get at the remaining angels, anxious to *uncreate* them, as well. Dalsa'in closed his eyes and prayed for some miracle that might rescue them. Without it, destruction would soon come for them all. He waited for the hand on his eyes to signal his doom.

Then, silence. Nothing happened.

He opened his eyes to see only his decimated band of angels. For one delirious moment, Dalsa'in thought the others had disappeared. The sound of wings above his head, however, told a different story.

Lucifer and the creatures had sprung upward toward the Well of Power.

CHAPTER TWENTY-ONE

"Fradyn, choose a small group of your best fighters, then you and Stondrin join me on the ledge for further instructions."

Michael motioned for Telsha'in and Grisson to follow him. They flew through the Mists of light and landed on the ledge, encircling the *Place of First Awareness*. After several moments, their task completed, Fradyn and Stondrin joined them.

"Here are the battle plans," Michael said. "As you've probably figured out by now, I'm splitting our forces." He glanced at Grisson. "My partner and I will lead the largest force through the black hole to attack Lucifer and his followers hard and fast. Because of their power to *uncreate*, we've got to keep them off-balance as much as possible."

He pointed to Stondrin. "I want you and the others to stay behind. For the moment, you will remain here in Heaven. You'll be the lookout for your group. Put yourself by the portal, but allow no more than the top of your head to protrude into the universe. I want you to *will* yourself to come out by the small rock next to the planet. With that little bit of yourself showing, no one below should be able to see you. But you'll be able to watch the action from that vantage point."

"What will I be watching for?" Stondrin asked.

"For a change, Stondrin, you've asked a good question." Michael smiled grimly. "You'll be watching and listening for me. Grisson or I will shout, 'For our Lord and our God!'" At that instant, you and Fradyn will come through the portal with your troops and attack the other side of Lucifer's forces."

Fradyn and Stondrin nodded their understanding. It sounded like a good plan.

"Telsha'in, you will stay here with Stondrin and the others. I want you to be the last one out of Heaven." Michael looked at the choirmaster to see if he heard. The angel inclined his head in agreement.

"Upon exiting Heaven, stand right beside the portal. During the battle, Grisson or I will shout, 'Behold, the music of Heaven!' That will be your cue to begin singing with all your might."

Telsha'in nodded again, but then asked, "What good do thing my singing will do?" Then his eyes widened as a thought came to him. "Or are you simply trying to keep me safe and out of the way?"

"This is too serious a matter to waste even one fighter," Michael said. "We already know Lucifer's creatures can't stand the light of Heaven. I'm hoping the music of Heave will have the same effect on them. And Telsha'in, you're the best in all of God's Country at praising our God in song."

The choirmaster stood as tall as possible and smiled. "I'll do my best."

Michael looked at the others. "With three different stages of attack, we just might pull this off and rid the universe of a foul disease."

"Let's do it," Fradyn said. The others chimed in their approval, as well.

"Inform your troops of what we'll be doing," Michael ordered Fradyn. "Stondrin and Telsha'in, go with him. I'll join you in a minute."

After they left, Michael turned to Grisson. "I want you to know several things before we leave Heaven."

The little angel had a feeling he knew what was coming.

"There's a good possibility we will lose this battle," Michael said.

"I'd thought as much," Grisson replied, shivering.

"But I want you to keep two things uppermost in your mind while in that dark universe. First, never leave my side. If we're going to survive, it has to be together. Our abilities complement each other. Your speed and my strength together will stop a lot of creatures.

"Second, God doesn't do things in a haphazard fashion. You were created for a special reason. So no matter how bad things may look, stay faithful to your purpose."

Embarrassment clouded Grisson's face. "It pains me to remind you again . . . but I don't have a purpose, Michael."

The archangel snorted in annoyance. "You can't use that as an excuse any longer. God knew what He was doing when he created you without a purpose. If you can't be faithful to your purpose, then remain faithful to your Creator." He looked long and hard at Grisson. "Remain faithful," he repeated.

"I'll try." Grisson swallowed hard. He was tired of change and chaos. How he longed for a little peace! "I'll do my best for God. I promise," he said.

"Let's go, then."

Michael dove off the ledge. Grisson followed close behind.

They found the troops assembled in teams. Fradyn's group had separated from the others, ready to do their part when called for.

"Is everyone ready?" Michael asked.

A chorus of assent flooded over him as the angels responded with enthusiasm.

"For our Lord and our God!" Michael roared.

The others echoed him. All of Heaven rang with their cry. "For our Lord and our God!"

Michael led the way through the portal, Grisson at his side. The other angels streamed through behind him. They flew into the dark universe, swifter and more deadly than lightening. The angels could barely see the black hole's dimness before them. Then, they were through it and the Well of Power floated beneath them.

Lucifer looked up, startled. With a snarl, he rose to meet them. Cruel-looking creatures fanned out behind him to come to Lucifer's aid.

His heart in his throat, knowing he would probably be destroyed, Grisson raced to the attack.

CHAPTER TWENTY-TWO

"Hold your troops, Michael," Lucifer ordered. "As you ought to be able to figure out, we're quite prepared to meet your attack."

He watched as Michael held up a restraining hand. Waves of angels massed up close behind the archangel, ready to do their leader's bidding. Their sheer numbers might very well overwhelm him. But now they looked so *puny* next to his own creatures.

He could see Grisson whispering to Michael . . . . Grisson! How could he still be alive? That one knew the fallen angels had been busy during his absence. Michael shook his head several times as Grisson continued talking. Now and then Michael gestured at one or another of the creatures, as if asking for confirmation that it had actually once been an angel.

Lucifer swelled with pride at what he'd accomplished in this re-creation. His creatures might be huge and bulky, but their size didn't hinder them when it came to speed. Their reaction time in responding to the sudden appearance of Michael and the angels had been astonishing. Finally Grisson broke off whispering. Michael nodded in agreement, but he didn't seem comfortable with whatever decision they'd reached.

Lucifer tried to ready himself for the events that would

unfold next. No one in Heaven or in this universe knew his old friend, Michael, better than Lucifer. And, he knew all of Michael's tricks. No, Lucifer would not to be taken by surprise. His confidence soared. His determination seemed matchless.

"We have nothing to say to each other, Lucifer." Michael sounded cold and formal. The raised hand holding back the angelic troops seemed ready to fall. Suddenly, Lucifer's confidence began to wane. Lucifer *thought* he could win the coming battle, but he didn't like the odds. Something had to be done to improve them.

Desperate, stalling for time until he could think of something, Lucifer said, "But Michael, think for a moment. We've been as one since the first light cycle of our creation. Surely we can work this out without anyone else being destroyed."

While Lucifer talked, his eyes scanned the forces ranged before his army. *This is the first time they've seen me since I began eating from The Well of Power*, he thought. *Look at them! Awestruck by my size and beauty! Maybe I can still enlarge my army and weaken Michael's forces at the same time.*

If, by some miracle – he grimaced, reminding himself not to use that word – Michael agreed to come and join him, the battle would be over. With his friend at his side, everything would be fine. No one could stand against a combination like that. No one.

That's it! Lucifer thought. *I'll offer him an honorable way out. He can keep Heaven for all his precious angels and give me the universe. No fighting, no one losing, continued friendship. That's why I deserve to rule,* he exulted to himself. *I always find a way to get what I want.*

Lucifer raised his voice, gathering in the watching angels with his eyes. When he was sure he had everyone's attention, Lucifer spoke the words his chosen path had earned him. Words that became the second-worst choice of his life. Words, though he could not know it at the time, that would separate Michael from him forever.

"Michael, are you okay?"

The archangel knew Grisson spoke to him, but he waved him away. Conflicting emotions flooded over Michael as he looked at the beautiful monstrosity before him. Lucifer had changed in every sense of the word. The dark angel's actions had unleashed evil in the universe and brought division into Heaven. He should attack. And yet . . . the opponent before him had been his friend for as long as he could remember. How could he hurt someone that close to his heart? His resolve wavered. His purpose suddenly seemed distant.

"What's wrong with everyone having whatever they want?"

The archangel could almost feel himself back before God's throne as Le Sage spoke those words of warning . . . . But those words hadn't come from the Throne Room!

Shock pulled him back to reality. The black universe swirled around him.

"What did you just say, Lucifer?"

Michael saw a small grin of triumph flit across his old friend's face.

"Why, you don't believe me?" Lucifer asked. "Allow me to repeat myself. There is a way everyone can have whatever they want − even you, Michael. So I ask you, What's wrong with everyone having whatever they want? Doesn't that make more sense that an all-out battle between old friends?"

Michael quit listening as his true purpose swam before his eyes. The intensity of his decision and the unexpected touch of God's love drove everything else away. God had known! He'd prepared for Michael's moment of weakness, even using it to make the archangel stronger. Even in His absence, God's will continued to prevail. The thought brought tears to Michael's eyes.

"The angels stay in Heaven. We stay here." Lucifer still pressed his argument. Michael realized this deceiver had misread the reason for the tears. His ego and pride now matched the size of his body!

"I'll give you the freedom to come talk with me from time to time – when I'm not too busy recreating this universe to suit my needs," Lucifer continued.

"Forget it, Lucifer. I've just been told to fulfill my purpose for God right here -- against you."

Michael could see Lucifer stiffen in anger. "What are you talking about?" his former friend demanded. "No one's given you any instructions since you've been here. And God has proven He isn't going to risk Himself in a battle with me." Lucifer raised a threatening fist toward Grisson and the others. "Show me who is trying to break up our friendship and I'll destroy him!" he shouted.

Now Michael glanced at Grisson out of the corner of his eyes. He wanted the little angel to pay close attention to the conversation, to learn that God still directed these events, even if they couldn't see Him.

"My purpose, " Michael continued, "is to fight you, Lucifer, and stop the bizarre creatures that follow you. From the moment we first came into *being*, created by God, I've been training for this day -- though I didn't know when or against whom I'd be fighting until now." He paused to consider his next words. "I'm not going to compromise what I know to be the truth. Nothing, not even your offer of safety and friendship, can keep me from loving and serving God in the best way I know how."

Then Michael laughed out loud. How good it felt to be free of indecision and fear!

"Lucifer, if you want to destroy the one who gave me instructions to fight you, then you'll have to destroy yourself! The words came from your own lips, placed there by your desire to rule in the place of God. Long before any of this occurred, God prophesied that the person who spoke those words would be my enemy. Never could I have imagined it would be you."

His eyes grew cold again. "You're no friend. You're a murderer and a liar."

The words, flung into the blackness of space between them, seemed to silence everyone. Lucifer grew pale. He looked at

Michael through half-slit eyes for a long moment. "So be it," he finally muttered. Then he turned his back on Heaven and Michael's friendship forever.

"What about you others?"

With great difficulty, Lucifer managed to ignore Michael and focus on the angels waiting to attack his followers. "By now, you must know our strength and unique powers will overpower every single one of you. Look at us! We're giants compared to the largest of you." Lucifer cast a contemptuous glance at Michael as he said this. "If you persist in attacking us, I'll personally make sure *none* of you exist after this battle."

Dismay spread throughout Michael's troops at these words. Luther pressed his advantage. "We angels have been created to live for eternity. It would be a shame to snuff out your potential for happiness." He looked around as the implication of what he said took effect. "Just think: if you *unbecome*, Heaven will never be a possibility for you again. Never to see the River of Light. Never to fly through the Mists toward God's throne. Never again to sail across the vast Ocean of Light. Do you truly want to risk all that?"

"If they follow you, they'll never have it again anyway!"

It surprised Lucifer to hear Grisson challenging him. Where had happened to his shy, unsure nature?

"Be honest with them, Lucifer," Grisson continued. "Tell them you can never go to Heaven again. Let them know if they follow you, they'll be changed into the same kind of grotesque monstrosities cringing behind you right now. Show them how the light of Heaven is now your deadly enemy. Tell them how that light, which once caressed your life and made it peaceful, is waiting to annihilate you. Tell them that darkness is now your home."

"He's right, Lucifer." Michael's comments added weight to the little angel's words. "If they follow you, they'll never see Heaven, God, or the River of Light. And, they'll have to live, along with you, in darkness forever."

Lucifer's face twisted in rage. The truth! He truly had a growing hate for that word. Look what it had accomplished. Now revulsion played across the faces of most of the angels.

But still, all was not lost. Lucifer had one more trick.

"Michael, I'm ashamed of you," he said with mock sorrow. "You have no confidence in some of your angels."

"What are you talking about, Lucifer?" He could tell Michael had tired of the stalling. The archangel wanted to get on with the battle and rid the universe of what he thought of as a sickness.

"Where are Toldin, Fradyn, Stondrin and the others? I know you wouldn't divide your forces and let them ambush us from the other portal, would you? After all, that wouldn't be very fair."

He grinned as the effect of his words hit Michael and Grisson. Both seemed stunned that he'd guessed their plan of attack. The surprise Michael counted on to help them win the battle had just been negated. Their chances grew slimmer with every passing moment.

"Don't you believe they have the fortitude to make their own decision about following me?" Lucifer continued. "If you're asking them to sacrifice their lives for your small-minded cause, shouldn't they have the right to decide for themselves whether it's worth *unbecoming* or not?"

If he was right, Michael would bring the other angels out from their hiding place. Now that Lucifer had destroyed the element of surprise, the best Michael could hope to accomplish would be to have the hidden troops as close to the scene of battle as possible. At least, that's what he would have done in Michael's place.

"Stondrin," Michael shouted. "Tell the other angels who'll be fighting to come out now." *Michael, you're playing right into my hands, and you don't even know it.* Lucifer struggled to keep his face impassive as events moved in his favor.

Lucifer's minions gawked as the last company of Michael's angels flew out of the silver portal and took up positions beside the small body orbiting the planet below. Lucifer could hear the uneasy mutters behind him as his creatures recalculated the odds of winning. They now knew the other side had far more numbers than did they. The time had come for him to strike.

"Toldin!" Lucifer called out.

The powerful angel flew out from the ranks. "What do you want, Lucifer?" he asked. Dislike dripped from every word spoken.

"Will you follow me and live?" Lucifer replied. He refused to acknowledge Toldin's hostility.

"I'll never follow an evil murderer like you. You'll have to destroy me if you ever want to live in this universe."

Well, thought Lucifer, *this one will be a good example.*

"I challenge you to a fight between just the two of us," he said. "These other angels need to understand what they're up against. They need to see that they're entering into a conflict your side cannot hope to win. You can help them make a wise decision." He spoke with condescension. "I promise not to hurt you or break anything."

"Never mind, Toldin. Lucifer's just trying to goad you into a fight you can't win." Michael's eyes shone like cold silver. "I forbid this fight to take place."

"We're not in the cavern playing at fighting anymore," Lucifer retorted. "This is the real thing: living for eternity or *unbecoming*. You're in *my* universe, Michael, and we'll fight according to *my* rules."

The former angel reached into The Well of Power and drew out a handful of the shining essence. "Don't let him hit you with what he's got in his hand!" Grisson shouted to the watching angels.

Lucifer drew back and threw the Well's substance directly at Michael. At the same time, he leaped farther and faster than anyone thought possible. Michael ducked straight under the power as it shot past him and disappeared harmlessly into the darkness. But when he reoriented himself toward Lucifer,

Michael was dismayed to see that the enemy of God no longer flew alone. Toldin struggled mightily to get away, but Lucifer held him with both hands.

"Now, Toldin," Lucifer purred. "We'll either have that fight you and I discussed earlier, or I'll destroy you on the spot."

Toldin nodded his head. "Like you said, *former angel*, this isn't like play fighting in the cavern. I believe you'll find my reflexes much sharper when my *being* is on the line."

At the words *former angel*, Lucifer winced; but he forced himself to put on a casual smile. Then he flew back several wing lengths and motioned toward Toldin. "I'll wager you find my reflexes and strength a good bit changed, as well. Attack, if you dare."

Toldin paused for a moment, then he shot forward at tremendous speed, engaging Lucifer. His reflexes shifted into high gear and he rained a series of swift blows on his opponent. For his part, Lucifer floated motionless. He tried neither to block the blows nor return them. The casual smile playing on his face never wavered.

As the fight progressed, Toldin threw even more of himself into the powerful blows. He struck his adversary in the face and chest. Nothing he could do, however, seemed to make the slightest change in Lucifer's demeanor.

Finally, Toldin tired and moved back a pace, out of Lucifer's reach. "This just proves it will take more than one of us to bring you down," he said. Toldin's breath now came in huge pants as he tried to regain his strength. "You've won nothing by this example."

"Oh no. You're wrong. I'm using you to imprint an indelible lesson on these others." The smile on Lucifer's face grew broader. "And one more thing. When I said I wasn't going to hurt you, I lied. You made a very wrong decision and you're going to pay . . . right now!"

No one but Grisson could follow Lucifer's next move. The dark angel lunged forward, closing the space between Toldin and himself instantly. Then he punched the angel full in the chest.

The blow didn't seem as if it landed very hard, but a look of agony swept over Toldin's face. He began to grow transparent. A scream ripped through the immediate area and, before anyone could take it in, Toldin disappeared from existence.

"What? . . . ." someone blurted out, then stopped. The angels had never before actually seen another angel *unbecome*. They had heard about it. But seeing their friend vanish before their very eyes was another thing entirely.

"Every one of my followers has the power to do the same thing! I have given them the ability to make you *unbecome*," Lucifer threw into the silence. "Now, I ask you again, who will follow me?"

Rumbling began in the angels' ranks as they discussed Lucifer's offer. Most of them shook their head and turned from their former friend in disgust. Others, however, seemed lost in thought, not at all sure of what they should do. A voice suddenly stood out above the rumbling--

"I've made up my mind."

Grisson turned to see Shi'intor move toward Lucifer. As he did so, angels from almost every company separated themselves and followed him. Only Shi'intor looked around at Michael as they left. His eyes shone with hatred. The other angels kept their eyes averted, ashamed of their cowardice.

"How can you do this, Shi'intor?" Michael pleaded. "Never to see Heaven or God again is a horrible sacrifice."

"You are leading everyone to their doom" Shi'intor spat back. "Destroyed, I'll never see Heaven again. But staying alive gives me the possibility of one day getting used to Heaven's light and returning."

"But Lucifer has set himself against God!" Grisson interjected. "Don't you care about your Creator?"

Shi'intor remained unmoved. "God doesn't care anything about us or He'd be here. So why should I fight for Him?" He looked at Grisson in disdain. "Besides, why should I listen to a scrawny angel who doesn't even know his own purpose? You ought to shut your mouth and fade back to wherever you came from."

Grisson swallowed hard and looked down, ashamed. Now everyone knew God had not given him a purpose. He wanted to hide from all the curious eyes now turned toward him.

Shi'intor flew to the side of his new leader, pleased with how he'd affected Grisson. He looked the former angel square in the eyes and said, "I'm ready to help you defeat these small-minded angels."

Lucifer withdrew several handfuls of power and flung them on the assembled group. The change was horrifying in its suddenness. Beauty disappeared, as evil took its place. The former angels grew larger and stronger. In but a few moments, hundreds of new monsters filled the space where there used to be beautiful beings of light.

Michael had seen enough. "For our Lord and our God . . . ATTACK!"

CHAPTER TWENTY-THREE

Michael's troops charged toward Lucifer and The Well of Power. Fradyn, hard-eyed following the loss of Toldin, led his angels downward from the dimly-glowing silver slash. They closed toward the fallen angels like two sharp blades of scissors, anxious to cut them down and end the battle quickly.

As they narrowed the distance between them and their enemies, however, Grisson wore a frown. Something wasn't right. "Michael," he said in an undertone. "Lucifer's not moving his creatures into position. We'd better be ready for another surprise."

"You're right," Michael responded. "But what it is I can't imagine." He slowed his speed, forcing those behind to do the same. As he examined the area, however, nothing seemed out of the ordinary. "Grisson, keep a sharp lookout and let me know the moment you see anything that can even remotely be used as a weapon against us. Otherwise, we have no choice but to continue the attack."

He increased his speed. At this rate both groups of angels would arrive at The Well of Power simultaneously. Lucifer would have to make a choice as to which group he engaged. The other, left free, could attack at will. Michael thought it a perfect plan . . . except for the unexpected.

When they were but a few hundred yards away, all could see Lucifer smiling and the creatures massed behind him relaxed and smug. Then the self-proclaimed master of the universe opened his mouth and released the black horde. Shrieking, grinding, blacker even than the darkness in which they worked their destruction, the droplets shot toward the unsuspecting angels.

"Get back!" shouted Grisson. "There's nothing you can use against that black horde. Those droplets will burn every part of you they touch."

The particles of mist quickly proved him right. They plunged into Fradyn's group and began burning holes in bodies and wings. Consternation replaced assurance. The formation of angels broke apart. Those pursued by the black droplets panicked. In their haste and terror, they slammed into other angels, making a larger, easier target for Lucifer's weapon.

"Grisson!"

The little angel turned to see a strange expression on his friend's face. Surprise and exultation warred for supremacy. "God is faithful, Grisson," Michael said. "He never leaves us without hope."

"What are you talking about?" Grisson asked. For a moment, he thought his friend had gone over the edge. How could he be happy in the midst of the chaos that reigned among his troops? Then . . . "Angels, look to me," the archangel shouted. He raised his right hand, palm outward. A brilliant white light exploded from the center of his palm. The creatures behind Lucifer moaned and covered their eyes in the face of such a reminder of Heaven. As the light reached the area of the black mist, it broke apart. Separate beams hunted down individual droplets. When they met, a blinding flash obliterated the droplet.

"Watch Lucifer," Michael commanded.

With each mini explosion, with each disappearance of a black droplet, Lucifer flinched as if he'd been hit. It was the first time Grisson could remember seeing him in any kind of pain since his transformation. As the explosions increased, holes began appearing in the former angel's body and he seemed to shrink a bit.

Michael sent out another burst of light. It hit Lucifer in the chest and drove him backward, slamming him against the Well. A third burst from Michael arrowed toward his enemy's head. Lucifer managed to crouch behind the Well and felt, rather than saw, the light absorbed into The Well of Power. A last explosion, and the black mist was no more. Its master cringed behind the only shelter he could find, and his minions milled about in uncertainty.

Michael sent out a final burst of light that enveloped those wounded by the black mist. Where the light touched, healing began. Burns vanished; holes disappeared; strength returned.

"Angels, hear me well," Michael shouted. "Our God gave me these powers not long ago. He knew this battle would take place and so provided this for our protection. Take heart. Finish the battle."

"All praise to God!" the angels cheered. They massed behind the archangel, ready to attack.

"It won't be that easy!" Lucifer might be hiding behind the Well, but he refused to give up. Caving in to Michael and his troops meant Lucifer would be forced out of existence, at worst. Even the best scenario saw him losing all his power, and Lucifer would not let go of even one droplet. He'd come to realize this wealth of power was a seductive drug that gave him a high he never wanted to lose.

Lucifer snaked out an arm, reached into the Well and drew out some power. He swallowed it, and watched in relief as the holes in his body closed rapidly. All might not be lost after all.

Lucifer swallowed yet another handful – and gained new knowledge and strength.

With a confident smirk again on his face, he stood up and faced Michael.

"This changes nothing," Lucifer said. "Your God is still a coward. He refuses to fight His own battles because He's afraid of me."

By way of an answer, Michael raised his hand again and released Heaven's light. This time, however, Lucifer remained motionless as the beam bore toward him. When it hit, the light slid off, as if coming against an invisible barrier.

"You see," Lucifer taunted. "The Well of Power gives me everything I want."

"Everything but my friendship," countered Michael. "That and fellowship with God are denied you forever."

Lucifer's beautiful face twisted in hatred. This time, it was he who shouted the words, "Come, my servants. ATTACK AND DESTROY!"

CHAPTER TWENTY-FOUR

Lucifer turned toward Michael as Heaven's defenders and Lucifer's followers slammed into one another at full speed. One of Lucifer's clans of creatures managed to isolate an angel. They swarmed over the being of light, each one touching him on the face and forehead. Their yell of triumph mixed with the angel's cry of despair as he *unbecame*.

The Great Battle had begun.

The dark angel saw his nemesis turn toward the group and unleash Heaven's light. It beamed straight for the group and hit them broadside. Two of the creatures disappeared. The third, bigger than his companions, was blown backwards. His shoulder hung awkwardly, and he moaned as he fell toward the planet below.

"You, you, and you. Come here!" Lucifer pointed to three of his most powerful creatures. "I want each of you to fly in a different direction. Make sure it's away from Michael." The hulking beasts before him nodded that they understood. "I've made sure you're each powerful enough to send an angel out of existence all by yourself." He turned them in the directions they were to fly. "I'll shield you from Michael's power. No one else is strong enough to stop you. Now, go!"

The three creatures shot out from behind The Well of Power. Lucifer headed straight for Michael. The other participants, on both sides, grappled with opponents who, in the recent past, had been good friends.

Michael saw the three huge former angels engaging his troops, but he was powerless to stop them. Lucifer bore down on him.

"Get behind me, Grisson," Michael ordered. Raising his hand, Michael unleashed the divine light. It slammed into Lucifer and brought him to a stop.

Michael and his opponent found themselves stymied. Neither could gain an advantage. Heaven's light and evil's strength kept both former friends from hurting the other. The moment Michael turned away to help another angel, Lucifer would be on him in a flash. Lucifer, however, was forced to maintain his position. If he left to help strengthen some of his groups, Michael would be free to turn his divine weapon on whomever he chose. But Lucifer seemed content to keep the contest between them a stalemate. When Michael risked a quick glance around, he understood why.

Wherever the three servants of Lucifer flew, chaos reigned. One touch by these creatures sufficed to make their target *unbecome*. None of the other angels seemed to know what to do. They saw their friends and comrades disappearing before their eyes and wanted to help them. But as soon as a group moved toward one of the monsters, another group of foul creatures swarmed over the would-be rescuers. A battle ensued invariably, with neither side winning. Meanwhile, however, Lucifer's three destroyers continued to wreak havoc and destruction.

"Your side is losing, Michael," Lucifer taunted. He saw a quick movement behind the archangel. "And tell your shadow, Grisson, that if he so much as moves a body length from you, I'll track him down and make sure he's the next to *unbecome*."

"Grisson, stay where you are." Michael's eyes never moved.

He continued to watch Lucifer. "Remember, we're staying together, partner."

Lucifer's visage turned pale for an instant. "Partner?" he sneered. "You've made that weakling your partner?" He dismissed the little angel with a derisive gesture. "Michael, your desperation is pitiful!"

Michael didn't let his attention wander for even an instant. "This 'weakling' had no trouble beating you, as I recall," he said.

"I'd be willing to let him try me again right now, unless you're afraid to lose your *partner*." Menace filled Lucifer's words. "I don't care how quick he is, I'll cut him into little pieces."

The huge angel of darkness let out a mighty roar. "You could have had *me* at your side. Together, we could have ruled the universe – *my* universe. Instead, you've teamed up with the angel who will go down in history as the creature having the shortest life-span ever!"

"I'll be glad to fight you, spawn of evil!" The words flew from behind Michael. Grisson's tone surprised him. "We can end this right now, if you wish . . . and it'll only take a moment for me to finish you off forever." Grisson sounded colder than the archangel had ever heard him.

"You, fight me?" Lucifer snorted. "And beat me? Angels aren't supposed to lie." A feral look swept across his face. "Not thinking about joining me, are you Grisson?"

The little angel moved from behind Michael. Flying beside the archangel, confronting Lucifer, he looked smaller than ever. But Michael could see no fear on his face.

"Angels don't lie, failed being of light," Grisson called out. "I meant what I said. I'll take you on and strike you down in an instant.

"All I ask is that we fight our next battle in Heaven."

Grisson gestured toward the silver portal gleaming in the darkness. "The Eternal Country is but a few beats of a wing away. Let's fly there, Lucifer."

His eyes bore into those of Lucifer. "Remember the beauty

of Heaven? Let's return to where light is everywhere. I'll fight you by the Mists of Light." He paused for a moment as his words sank in. "We can let you fade from existence right beside the *Place of First Awareness*, where you came into being because of God's love for you. Come on, let's go."

Lucifer froze in his place.

"If you're so powerful, you'll be able to handle the light of Heaven," Grisson continued. "After all, I'm just a little, new angel. If I can exist in the light, surely you can as well." His eyes widened then, as if a surprising thought had occurred to him. "But you can't return to Heaven, can you? I guess that means you're weaker than any of the angels of God."

Grisson pointed a finger at his Accuser. "You're actually weak and a coward at heart! That's why you're obsessed with being bigger and more powerful than anyone else. Because you're afraid!"

No sound came from Lucifer. He stared at Grisson with a terrible hatred. "Your *unbecoming* will be slow, indeed," he managed to choke out.

CHAPTER TWENTY-FIVE

The darkness seemed to deepen as more and more angels *unbecame*. Above them, cold planets and lifeless suns wobbled out of their orbits. Like a pebble thrown into a pool, the failing universe spread its sickness in ever-widening circles. Celestial bodies crashed into one another and exploded. The result tore mammoth chunks loose and hurled them everywhere, deadly shrapnel that threatened to punch planet-sized holes through everything in their path. Beneath the warring angels and creatures, Earth continued to disintegrate. Quakes racked its interior. Volcanoes proliferated, spawned by the anarchy that reigned and destroyed everything.

A cold smile played on Lucifer's face as he watched the battle unfold. Even when a group of angels managed to drag one of his followers to The Well of Power and throw him in, the Dark Angel showed no emotion. Grisson realized, once again, that Lucifer loved only himself.

"Are you ready to surrender?" The Dark Angel turned his attention back to his two tormenters.

Grisson watched as Michael shook his head in response to Lucifer's question.

"I'll never surrender. Even if I'm the last one to represent Heaven, my loyalty will always be to God."

"Don't you care for your angels?" Lucifer had calmed his voice once more.

"Look around you. Hundreds have already disappeared forever. Many more will *unbecome* before this light cycle is completed."

Lucifer switched his attention to Grisson. "I was angry at you earlier, but I'm over it now. Even to you I offer mercy. If you both refuse my offer, you condemn not only yourselves, but all your followers to Fradyn's fate." He swept his hand toward the center of the battle, drawing his and Michael's attention to the angel in question.

Fradyn flew into the thick of a melee between three angels and fifteen creatures who were about to *uncreate* them. Flinging his opponents left and right, he fought valiantly toward his imperiled friends. Fradyn saved his blows as he ducked punches and dodged kicks. Only when he could deliver a crippling stroke would he unleash his tremendous strength. With smashed knees, dislocated shoulders and blinded eyes, his enemies began to falter in their attack. The angels saw they had a rescuer, and began to battle with renewed strength. It looked as if Fradyn might pull off a miracle, after all.

He never saw the huge monster behind him.

"Fradyn, turn around!" Grisson shouted with all his might, but the sounds of battle drowned him out.

A forceful blow to Fradyn's side stunned the courageous angel. He managed to half-turn and tried to defend himself. Before he could even raise a hand, however, darkness filled his vision and he knew no more.

One of Heaven's bravest angels joined the ranks of the *uncreated*.

"There is no hope," Lucifer repeated. "You condemn more of your followers by hesitating. Nothing can – Unhh!"

Grisson's heart leaped with joy as the five angels struck the middle of Lucifer's back. Their combined power knocked him off balance. He began to fall as four more angels held his wings. The three monsters chosen by Lucifer to annihilate Heaven's forces found themselves suffocated by invading angels and suffering the same fate.

Michael looked about in amazement. "Where did these angels come from?" He whirled on Grisson. "Did you have reserves hidden that I knew nothing about?"

"I'd love to take responsibility," Grisson responded, "but I'm as much in the dark about this as you are."

"Sorry to be so long in coming," shouted Dalsa'in as he flew up from the planet's surface. "But we wanted to be sure Lucifer had forgotten about us being left behind on Earth." His angels flew into the battle with a vengeance, ready to help rid the universe of the evil that had threatened to wipe them out but a short while earlier.

"Dalsa'in, how did you and your group happen to be down there all this time?" Michael asked.

Dalsa'in's eyes turned a steely silver. "We were angels originally loyal to Lucifer and assigned to his service. When he transformed himself, we knew something had gone terribly wrong. His defiance of God made us realize we could never serve him."

The angel's head dropped as he thought about all that had happened on the dying planet. "Lucifer used us as practice for his monsters. They sharpened their deadly skills on my friends. I watched them *unbecome* before my eyes." He glanced down at the captured Lucifer as he sank toward Earth. "That poor excuse for an angel held me and made me watch the torture as it went on and on. Then he tried to blame everything that happened on *me*, saying it was my fault because I refused to give in to him."

Dalsa'in grasped Michael's shoulder. "Had you and the others not come when you did, we would have all been wiped out. You saved our lives."

"I think you just did the same for us," the archangel responded. "So, let's get to work."

Michael, now free from the responsibility of holding Lucifer at bay, raised his hand. Light pulsed from him three times. Each beam flew in a different direction. Three pulses, three directions, three roars of despair. When the light finally dissipated, the three monsters who had hurt so many were no more.

Cheering broke out in the ranks of angels. The tide of the battle began to turn. Individual angels joined up once again with their groups. Order returned as they methodically began working together. Angels isolated creatures, threw them off balance and then dragged them to The Well of Power and disposed of them.

We're going to win, Grisson thought. *We're going to make it back to Heaven.*

Lucifer twisted violently as he fell toward the planet. The nine angels who held him were hard-pressed to maintain their grip. He tensed his muscles and kicked a powerful leg all the way over his head. Two of the angels had to duck to avoid being struck. When they did, Lucifer managed to whirl around and grab them. His speed and strength were more than any of them had expected, and he caught them off guard.

This time, Lucifer wasted no time with words or boasts. He sent the two angels out of existence with stunning swiftness. Then the big dark angel reached behind him with both arms and tore away two more angels. They *unbecame*, as well. The others abandoned their task and attempted to fly upward toward Michael. One of them, however, was a little too slow. Lucifer grabbed him from behind. Rage flowed through his body as he saw his three weapons of destruction burned away by Heaven's light. He ripped the hapless victim before him in two before consigning him to *uncreation*.

"If they think the battle is over this easily, I've got a surprise for them," he muttered. For the first time since his transformation, Lucifer used every bit of his considerable speed and blurred toward The Well of Power.

The angels in LeSage's group struggled with their captive.

They outnumbered him four to one, but the monster's bulk made it hard for them to do much more than drag him toward the Well.

"Don't worry . . . about anything . . . but his arms and wings," LeSage panted. He and the others were worn out from fighting the monster's superior strength.

The former angel kicked out in frustration. He missed everyone, but made contact with The Well of Power. Pain flitted across his face and he froze for an instant. That was all LeSage and his team needed. They shoved in unison and the monster disappeared into the Well's depths. "That's the last good deed you'll ever do."

LeSage looked up to see Lucifer seemingly appear from nowhere and send his three companions out of existence in a flash. He choked convulsively as two hands grabbed his throat and squeezed.

"Your wisdom hasn't helped you very much, has it?" Lucifer whispered in the angel's ear. "Guess I can change your name to LeFool.

"You can save yourself by bowing to me. I'll give you first place in my kingdom. Your wisdom will be known throughout the universe." He pulled the angel up to him until their faces were almost touching. "What do you say to that offer?"

LeSage tried to move his head a bit to get some relief. "I do have wisdom, Lucifer. I've devoted all my existence to learning as much about God as I can." He forced himself to look into the very face of evil. "That same wisdom tells me you are doomed to failure. Do with me what you will, I'll never betray God's trust in me."

Lucifer's hands squeezed ever tighter. LeSage gurgled once, and vanished into nothingness.

"Michael, The Well of Power!"

The archangel responded to Grisson's warning. He turned from his attack on the creatures to see Lucifer *uncreate* LeSage. The dark angel moved faster than anyone had thought possible.

Hands scooping incessantly, he gorged himself with power from the Well. In the space of but a moment, more than twenty handfuls of energy went into his mouth. This time, however, Grisson could see no change in Lucifer. After consuming the power, he seemed no bigger or stronger.

Michael noticed the same thing. "Perhaps he's grown to his limit. At least, let's hope so." "I don't think that's the case," Grisson responded. "He seems to be able to control how he changes. I think he just added power we can't see."

Lucifer stood up from behind The Well of Power. "You're right, shrimp," he said.

The voice that had been so beautiful in Heaven now proved even more powerful and beguiling than before. Lucifer shouted, "Hear me, all of you!"

Angels and monsters ceased fighting and turned their attention to the Fallen One.

"I have a confession to make. Earlier, I had a moment of worry. The thought crossed my mind that you'd beaten me. But then I realized something like that could never happen, because *I'm too strong and smart to be defeated by the likes of you.*"

His eyes turned from black to a dark yellow. In their center, the darkness roiled and seethed like something alive. "Michael, I've prepared a little something for you. I think you'll find it quite entertaining."

He raised his hand, palm outward, aiming toward the archangel. Michael, out of reflex, did the same. Twin flashes of light and darkness burst from the two mighty warriors. When the beams met, an explosion of tremendous force followed the lines of energy back to Michael and Lucifer. The two greatest creations in all of Heaven and the universe were blown backwards like blades of grass in a hurricane. The explosion knocked them off their feet and sent them tumbling helplessly through space.

Grisson took advantage of the situation. "The Well of Power is free for the moment. Angels, continue your work!"

The beings of light responded with alacrity. Before their enemies could turn away from watching their fallen leader, they found themselves being dragged to The Well of Power and cast to their doom.

"Good job, angels!" Grisson continued to monitor the battle. "The moment you see Lucifer returning, however, abandon the Well and fly to my position."

Michael began regaining control of his flight with difficulty. He had no idea what had happened a few moments ago, but it had surely changed him. His body felt different. Something had . . . gone out of him. No time existed for further examination, however. He sped forward once more toward The Well of Power. A battle waited to be won.

Lucifer responded much more slowly. The explosion had slammed him into the planet's surface and now he found himself falling into one of the recently formed fissures. Steam hissed around him as it made its way upward from Earth's center. An ominous rumble seemed to come from everywhere. Massive stones shifted and with a groan, the fissure closed, entombing him. Deep within the bowels of the Earth, surrounded by rock, dirt and darkness, Lucifer sighed and lay back inside his unstable prison. Not even the slightest glimmer of light could find its way into these rocky depths, but he saw everything with perfect clarity.

"I'll bet Michael never expected anything like *that* to occur," he whispered in the darkness. A dangerous grin flitted across his face. "Now it's time for the finale." He spread his vast wings and sped through the strata of rock and stone that could not hold him.

The Well of Power, his drug of choice, awaited him.

CHAPTER TWENTY-SIX

Grisson couldn't understand how he had gotten in this position.

Only a few light cycles ago, he hadn't even existed. Now, with Michael temporarily out of commission, the little angel discovered he had a knack for understanding battle formations and strategy. As angels and foul creatures fought each other for control of the universe, Grisson directed his troops with calm and assurance. Where others might only see tangled groups of warriors, Grisson perceived the scope and flow of the whole battle. Shouting orders, moving stronger angels to places they were needed the most, he could see they were beginning to win the battle. It still pained him when a flash or scream indicated another angel had *unbecome*. But Grisson had the satisfaction of knowing far more of Lucifer's creatures were being flung out of existence as angels fed The Well of Power the universe's trash.

A streak of silver in the corner of his vision caused Grisson to turn his head. Michael had returned – and at full speed. But where Michael was –

"To me! Angels, to me *now!*"

The troops broke off their attack and sped toward their interim leader . . . and not a moment too soon. Lucifer burst from the center of the Earth with a roar on his lips and evil in his eyes. He flew to The Well of Power and stopped directly behind it.

"Come to me, my servants," he commanded. His followers seemed only too glad to obey him. They crowded in behind Lucifer, making sure to keep him between them and the hated Well.

"Here we are again," Lucifer said to Michael. "Isn't this how we began this whole conflict: your troops with you on one side, mine with me on the other?"

Michael appraised his troops. He knew every angel fighting for him. "There's a difference, Lucifer. It looks like Heaven's side lost far fewer of its faithful than you did. I have a feeling you're not going to like how the rest of the battle plays out."

To the archangel's surprise, Lucifer threw his head back and laughed. "And I think you've yet to understand what happened between the two of us during that explosion." A moment later, he turned serious. His mercurial moods were becoming worse. "You're going to lose, Michael. You and all your weak-minded puppets are doomed. The time for talking is finished," he snarled. "Do your worst, if you dare."

The archangel raised his hand and pointed it toward the dark angel. The creatures behind Lucifer shaded their eyes. They wanted to keep themselves from being blinded by the intense light. Some whimpered as they waited for the flash and the burning that accompanied it.

But nothing happened. No light shone forth from the leader of Heaven's angels.

"How do you like my little surprise, Michael? It cost me a lot, but it was worth it." Lucifer began eating from The Well of Power once again. His followers raised hands and hooves as they roared their approval of the sudden turn of events.

"Now the playing field is level," Lucifer gloated, looking at the stunned angels. "My black mist is gone; so is your divine light."

He turned toward his followers. "But you, my servants, still have the power to make these hated angels *unbecome*." Sweeping his arm forward, he commanded, "Finish the battle!"

The Eternal Country stood devoid of angels for the first time since their creation.

No one sat on the ledge at the *Place of First Becoming*. No wings beat above the River of Light. The falls roared their majesty in emptiness. But, the Ocean of Light still swirled and gathered power from below . . . and that power held purpose, as did everything in Heaven.

Was the roar of the falls a bit louder? Did the River of Light seem to be moving swifter? Light from the falls began growing in intensity as the Ocean of Light poured ever more celestial water from above. And then, from the falls, a pulse of light burst forth.

"What . . .?" Stondrin's head shot up and his eyes had a faraway look.

Grisson risked a glance around. Every other angel wore the same expression.

"I received a message from Heaven!" Stondrin said.

"So did I." "And so did I." Angels began talking excitedly to each other.

"Was it God?," Grisson asked.

Stondrin shook his head. "I couldn't tell. But I do know this. It was a command, and it came from the Eternal Country." His smile reflected the faces of every other angel – every angel but Grisson.

"What was the message?" the little angel asked, his stomach sinking as he realized he, again, had received no message.

Stondrin shook his head once more. "I'm not allowed to tell you right now. The time may come when I can share it with you, but I'm forbidden to do so at the moment." Other voices echoed the same thing. "But at least this gives us hope. Someone is still encouraging us."

"Not me," Grisson said with despair. "I heard nothing." But in the angels' excitement, no one paid attention to his words.

CHAPTER TWENTY-SEVEN

Telsha'in stood quietly beside the portal leading into Heaven. Sounds of fighting wafted up from the battlefield far below. Sometimes a scream would startle him. Each time, he prayed the angels would be protected.

The chief singer of Heaven had a gentle manner. Other angels said his eyes, always filled with compassion, seemed so caring that surely his real name had to be "Love," not Telsha'in. That same compassionate nature now tormented the angel. How he wished all the angels − even those who had fallen by following Lucifer − could put their differences behind them and be as one family again. If only God had not left . . . . Tears flowed down his face as he thought of the One who had given him the gift of song. The joy he used to experience at all times -- the joy he once took for granted − now seemed so far away.

How much longer would he have to wait? Would the angels even need his help? In any event, Telsha'in tried to keep himself prepared. He hummed several of the praise songs he'd composed for God. Remembering the words renewed his faith and gave him strength.

The battle sounds changed. Now, there were more and more screams. The few words he could make out chilled him to the bone. They were words of desperation, shouted by angels pleading for help.

Then, the words he'd both waited for and feared called him to action. He did not know it, but the next moments of his life would exact from Telsha'in a terrible price.

The Well of Power seemed to beckon to the angels. Only a few hundred meters away, it promised victory if the angels could but offer Lucifer's followers as a sacrifice upon that fearsome altar. In reality, however, The Well of Power might as well have been on the other side of the universe. With Michael's loss of the gift of Heaven's light, the battle had shifted in favor of Lucifer.

The teams of angels could hold their own against their opponents. But when they attempted to drag a creature to the Well, they found Lucifer waiting for them. Hovering always around his source of strength, he *uncreated* anyone who dared come close to The Well of Power. Nor could anyone lure him away. The Dark Angel refused to chase anyone, including Michael, if it meant moving from his base of safety.

The angels now found themselves in a terrible predicament. Without Heaven's light or The Well of Power, they had no way to send the creatures out of existence. Lucifer, on the other hand, had effectively blocked their way back to Heaven. He had stationed powerful creatures who *uncreated* any angels who tried to flee to a portal. It seemed as if all hope was gone.

"The end is near!" shouted Lucifer, confirming the angels' worst fears. "Come to me, angels, and I will spare your life. Abandon that loser you call a leader and join the winning side!" As he spoke, the creator of evil snaked out a hand and latched onto another angel who had thought himself far enough away from the Well to be safe. A quick touch, a flash, and the beings of light found their ranks thinner by one.

Michael and Grisson did their best to even the odds. The archangel's strength was such that two and sometimes three creatures at a time were beaten and stunned by his blows when they attacked. Grisson showed great courage following each fight. He would fly straight toward Lucifer at such speed that even that powerful creature had to defend himself. Each time, Lucifer came close to grabbing Grisson and making him *unbecome*. And each time, barely, Grisson escaped. For the few seconds it took to fight off the little angel, Michael would slip in with his stunned enemies and touch them to The Well of Power. Even that slight brush against God's power proved sufficient to send them out of existence.

But while Michael and Grisson were eliminating two or three, Lucifer's creatures *uncreated* twenty or more. No other team possessed the strength and speed of the archangel and Heaven's newest angel. So as the battle continued, Lucifer's confidence and arrogance increased. "Who will join me?" the Dark Angel repeated.

To their credit, no angels responded to his offer. But with each offer from Lucifer, their morale declined and their strength seemed to dwindle.

Wave after wave of foul creatures tested Michael and his partner. The archangel panted from the exertion. His breath came in great gasps. As soon as one group of monsters had been defeated, another took its place. Grisson flew behind the latest attacker and grabbed its wings. When he looked up at Michael, waiting to see how he would fell this one, the archangel shocked Grisson by shaking his head and pointing upward.

"What?" Grisson asked. He struggled to maintain his position. The monster used its considerable strength to begin pulling away.

Michael, still breathing heavily, managed to gasp out one word, "Telsha'in!"

"Angels," began Lucifer a third time. "Can't you see what . . .."

"That's enough, master of lies," Grisson interrupted. He let go of the monster and effortlessly dodged its attempts to capture him. "You're still worried about the battle's outcome or you wouldn't be so intent on getting us to quit and join you." He saw hope dawn in the eyes of the other angels as they understood the truth of his words.

"The battle is not yet over. We have more in store for those traitors who would betray God."

Lucifer's roar cut him off. "Words. That's all you offer. Angels are *unbecoming* even as you speak. You might delay the outcome by your stalling tactics, but in the end, all will know I'm invincible."

"Invincible?" The little angel moved closer to Lucifer, seemingly unafraid of his power. "Let's see just how strong you are."

Grisson took a deep breath and shouted with all his might, **"BEHOLD, THE MUSIC OF HEAVEN!"**

The strong, beautiful voice seemed to come from everywhere. Angels found hope in the words and music. Reflexes became speedier. Tired muscles developed new strength. Determination replaced despair in their eyes. And, as Telsha'in sang of God and His goodness, an amazing thing happened.

"No! Can't stand the pain!" Lucifer staggered back from The Well of Power, his hands over his ears. He moaned and shook his head, trying to clear away the agony caused by Heaven's music. The battle ceased to be important for him. His very survival seemed threatened by this new divine weapon.

A joyous shout pulled him out of his misery. Lucifer looked up to see hundreds of angels rushing at him. With his new vision, he could also see the battles taking place with his followers. And all of them were losing. His creatures were as weakened and in pain as their leader. They offered no resistance as angels swarmed over them and dragged them to the Well and to their doom.

"It's not over yet, Michael," he shouted, trying to ignore the pain. "You're not the only one with surprises." The Dark Angel stood his ground as the celestial horde rushed toward him. Just before they reached their evil prey, Lucifer laughed once, glanced at Michael . . .

And vanished.

"How did he do that?" Grisson asked.

"Even more important than that, where did he go?" Michael looked about grimly, but Lucifer had effectively disappeared.

"Grisson, these creatures should pose no problem to us now. I want you to continue to direct our forces. I'm going to try to find the coward. If he went where I think he did, we're all in trouble."

The little angel nodded that he understood, and turned to direct and help out where needed. Michael took flight, desperation lending speed to his wings.

Telsha'in sang on, wondering if his music made a difference. It might be his imagination, but it seemed as if the universe was less dark than before. He watched as, far below, the Earth steadied some in its rotation. Perhaps all of God's creation responded in some way to praise offered with a sincere heart to the Heavenly Father.

Lucifer exploded from nowhere to float before him.

Telsha'in showed his courage at that moment. Instead of fleeing or faltering, the singer stood his ground and sang even louder. This close, the effect on the Dark Angel was stunning. He fell backwards and grew thinner as the music pounded into him.

Concentrating, Lucifer tried to remember his plan. Eyes squeezed shut. One hand covered an ear. His head lowered as he tried to use a shoulder to cover the other ear. That left one hand free. Blindly, he swung his fist in a mighty arc. It caught Telsha'in in the side and caused him to lose his breath.

Lucifer straightened and tried to regain his composure. He had but a moment of wonderful silence in which to work. Telsha'in backed away from him. The angel bent over, trying to regain his voice as quickly as possible.

The master of evil laughed as strength flowed back into him. In a moment, the singer would never sing again. He started toward Telsha'in, but the angel's eyes flicked to the left. Lucifer risked a quick glance in that direction, just in time to see a pair of feet aimed at his face.

As strong as he had become, even Lucifer could not withstand a blow from Michael, delivered at full speed, feet first. A line of fire shot through his jaw and he felt teeth give way. Sluggishly, he tried to fly away. Michael had his wings immobilized.

"Sing, Telsha'in," Michael commanded. "We'll see how much courage this fallen angel has when confronted by someone who can really hurt him."

Telsha'in began another song of praise to God. A groan escaped Lucifer's lips as the song and Michael hit him at the same time. He could feel his former friend – and often his equal in battle – attempting to pull one of his wings out of socket.

"The pain . . . the pain . . . . Please stop. I beg you . . ."

If he could just get a hand behind him, he'd rip Michael in two. Lucifer tried to think how to proceed. He knew the music wouldn't kill him. And The Well of Power happened to be too far away for even Michael and Telsha'in to try to drag him against his will. With enough patience and stamina, they'd make a mistake and then . . . .

"Let's drag him into Heaven."

Trust Michael to find the one thing he had overlooked! Lucifer felt himself being moved forward. The silver slash burned in his vision. Even here, in the universe, his skin began to bubble and rupture from the little bit of light escaping the portal. Panic rose up in him. It couldn't end like this! Think, he snarled at himself. But the silver grew brighter. The portal seemed to open wide, a giant maw ready to consume him. He struggled wildly, but to no avail. The music grew louder, the pain more intense. Smoke curled up from his eyes . . . .

Michael found himself holding a few feathers. Telsha'in discovered he sang only to the archangel.

Lucifer had vanished once more.

CHAPTER TWENTY-EIGHT

The deepest shade of darkness existing in the universe caressed and smoothed. The lone inhabitant of the black hole moaned as he floated in the thick, inky blackness. Lucifer sighed deeply and reveled in cold night that acted as a balm to his tortured body. Burns healed; bruised wings strengthened.

As his power returned, Lucifer turned his mind to the problem at hand. Telsha'in had to be stopped or the battle would be lost. The singing of God's choirmaster, Lucifer admitted to himself, had been a factor he'd not counted on when planning the overthrow of Heaven. There had to be a way to neutralize the singer. If he could just get Telsha'in away from that cursed entrance into Heaven . . . .

That was it!

Lucifer bared his sharp teeth in an evil grin of triumph. "Dear Michael," he whispered, "have I got a surprise for you!"

"You don't have to stay here with me," protested Telsha'in. "I'll be all right as long as I stay right next to the portal." He paused to look toward the planet far below. "Besides, there's a battle whose outcome depends on you."

Michael shook his head. "Without Lucifer's presence and with your singing, we'll win the battle handily enough. Right now, you're our most potent weapon." He edged closer to the choirmaster. "The best thing I can do is make sure you're able to continue singing."

Telsha'in pointed to Michael's right. "What's that?" he asked.

A dark, vertical line began to form in front of the singer.

"Move back, now." Michael had become wary of anything that hinted of darkness. When Telsha'in didn't move fast enough, the archangel reached out to pull him closer to the silver slash that acted as Heaven's doorway. Before he could make contact, however, a powerful arm shot through the dark line and grabbed the singer by the throat.

Telsha'in made a choking sound and waved his hands ineffectually. The arm snatched him back through and both disappeared.

"Lucifer must have created his own portal," Michael said to himself. He had no idea where it led or what lay on the other side. But he never hesitated. With a tremendous surge of his wings, he jumped through Lucifer's doorway of darkness.

CHAPTER TWENTY-NINE

Michael exited the portal and found himself close to the black hole God the Son had used as a shortcut through the universe. He was just in time to see Lucifer and Telsha'in disappear into the terrible darkness. With a sigh, he hurried to make up the distance. They couldn't afford to lose the choirmaster and hope to win the battle easily.

He charged through the black hole at top speed. For a moment, oppressing gloom surrounded him, then the archangel burst through to the other side and saw the first portal God had created gleaming in the distance. Around him stretched the emptiness of space, punctuated only by a star off to his right. Nothing moved as far as the eye could see.

Just to make sure, Michael flew around the star to see if he could surprise anyone using it as a hiding place. As he suspected, however, he found himself alone.

Lucifer and Telsha'in were somewhere in the black hole. And Michael had no way of seeing into that vast hiding place. He shook his head in sorrow for his friend. It looked as if the sole help he could now offer lay close to The Well of Power. He turned his back on the portal that pointed the way toward Heaven and home. His troops needed him.

Stondrin and Grisson fought together as another foul creature went into nothingness. Both angels had lost their teammates. Stondrin's had *unbecome*; Grisson's partner had -- he hoped -- flown away to help Telsha'in.

The fighting continued unabated. Around The Well of Power, horned monsters and beings of light grappled with one another. Neither side seemed willing to give up. With the absence of Telsha'in's singing, the huge advantage held by the angelic forces shrank once again.

"Watch out behind you!" Grisson called out. Stondrin whirled just in time to avoid a taloned fist aimed at his head. The creature drew back for another try when a foot crashed into the side of his neck. Grisson pulled back his leg and grimaced. "Those scales are tough."

Stondrin grabbed for the creature's legs as it hung before him, stunned by Grisson's kick. The little angel immobilized their captive's wings and turned to begin the short journey to The Well of Power.

A group of three creatures flew in front of them and cut them off. Stondrin looked around. All the other angels were engaged in their own fights. To make it worse, the monster he and Grisson held had come out of its stupor. Writhing and twisting about, it snarled imprecations at them, warning of what it would do if escape ever became a possibility.

"We'll help you, Lyma'al," rasped one of the creatures. They swept forward as one toward the two angels.

"Fly away, Grisson!" Stondrin had already let go of Lyma'al's feet and prepared to escape. Grisson, with great difficulty, used the monster's wings to swing it around and thrust it in the path of the would-be rescuers. Instead, showing incredible agility, the monster whirled back around and swiped at Grisson's head. The little angel's reflexes still operated well, however. He dropped under the murderous stroke and backpedaled toward Stondrin. They would be lucky to escape with their lives.

"I can't do all this by myself, you know. Even I need a little help."

The voice came from behind the four creatures.

"Michael!" Grisson grinned from ear to ear. "Here we come."

The archangel head-butted one creature. Then, using its shoulders for support, he kicked back and upwards at the same time. His feet caught two more creatures on the point of their chins, and knocked them out at the same instant.

The remaining monster, Lyma'al, found itself suddenly alone. It half-turned just in time to see a foot slam into its neck.

Grisson pulled his leg back and grimaced. "Isn't this how we began this whole thing?"

Stondrin nodded to Michael in gratitude. "You sure showed up at the right time." He helped the other two angels drag their opponents to The Well of Power and send them out of existence.

"Where have you been?" Grisson asked.

"No time for that now." Michael drew the two angels close to him. "Lucifer is somewhere in the black hole with Telsha'in. If he *uncreates* our choirmaster and returns here, we can forget about winning this battle." Grisson nodded in agreement. To give Lucifer further access to The Well of Power would be suicide.

"My problem is that I can't see inside the black hole," Michael continued. "Can either of you think of a way to find Lucifer in his dark hiding place?"

Grisson looked around at the battle that continued unabated. All the angels confronted a determined group of monsters. A flash still occurred from time to time, indicating an angel's *unbecoming*. For the most part, however, the angels had the upper hand. Slowly, inexorably, they pressed their advantage of numbers over the dark powers of Lucifer's followers. It would take time, but if they could keep the odds the same, they would win.

"We can't spare any angels to help search through the black hole," he observed.

"No, we'd need too many for that," agreed Michael. "I couldn't send any angel by himself through that darkness to look for Lucifer. To be effective, we'd need teams of fifteen or twenty apiece." He sighed in frustration. "There doesn't seem to be anything we can do."

Stondrin got a faraway look in his eyes. "It's a long shot, but I just might have a solution to our problem." I've been curious about something that happened earlier and"--

The others laughed. "Trust Stondrin to still be curious even as our very existence is on the line," Michael said, grinning.

Stondrin blushed. "I know. But that's a part of my purpose. Maybe God created me just so my curiosity would work at this moment. Anyway . . . . "

Telsha'in trembled as the cloying darkness seemed to press in on him. His eyes could see nothing. He could sense a hand around his throat. He heard the voice of evil in his ear.

"Now you will learn of my power, choirmaster."

Telsha'in tried to reply, but the hand closed tighter about his throat. It choked off all sound. He prepared himself for *unbecoming*.

"I'm not going to *uncreate* you, because you're no longer a threat to me," the voice whispered.

Telsha'in felt a thick finger touch his vocal chords once. A wave of nausea swept over him. Then the choking hand pulled back and he felt blessed relief.

"Sing, if you wish," the voice taunted. "Call to your friends and ask to be rescued." A cruel laugh sounded beside his ear.

Telsha'in opened his mouth to sing – and only a weak "croak" came out. Horrified, he cleared his throat and tried again. But the results were the same.

"Lucifer," He could barely make a sound. "What have you done to me?"

"I told you," said the evil one. "I've shown you my power.

"Now," he continued in a softer, nicer tone. "You know I could have *uncreated* you. But my love of you and your music has always been such that I would deplore robbing all creation of your unique gift."

"You've already done that," Telsha'in managed to whisper.

"But not forever. Not even for a long while – if you'll agree to sing for me and my kingdom." Lucifer patted the singer's shoulders in what he hoped the singer would interpret as a comforting gesture. "Sing only for me, and you'll have your same voice back in but a moment." He tried to sound as loving as possible. "What do you say to my generous offer?"

One part of Telsha'in's mind heard what Lucifer said. His thoughts, however, were in God's Throne Room. He heard again God asking him what might be the most important thing for the choirmaster. At that time, Telsha'in had responded by saying, "Singing for You." God had seemed displeased with the singer's response, but the 'why' of it had been missing until this moment.

Telsha'in formed his words carefully. He knew how difficult and painful it would be to say his next words. But at the same time, his heart felt strangely light and at peace.

"It is more important for me to be faithful to God than it is for me to sing," he declared. "I want to sing, with all my heart. But if it can't be for God, then let my silence speak of His glory."

"So be it," Lucifer snapped. "I'll not *uncreate* you because you're now of no consequence to the outcome of this battle." He ground his teeth in frustration. "I leave you here to find your own way out of the darkness – if you can. I'm returning to The Well of Power – and to victory."

Lucifer laughed as he moved away from the impotent singer. "Nothing can stop me now."

"Are you sure you were standing here when he threw it?"

Michael nodded, impatient to go. "Yes, I'm sure." He pointed to the side of the planet below. "The essence from The Well of Power passed right over my head and disappeared in that direction."

"If it didn't hit anything, it could still be traveling," Stondrin explained once again. "Let's see if we can catch up with it."

Without waiting for the others, Grisson shot in the direction indicated by the archangel. Something deep within his breast seemed to drive him. His wings blurred through the universe; soon, the planet, The Well of Power and other angels lay far behind.

Past the Earth stretched nothing but empty space. Grisson strained his eyes to scan the black curtain before him. A tiny twinkle of light appeared for an instant far ahead and to the right.

"I've found it," he called back to the others. "More to the right; follow me."

He dove for the light that became ever brighter. As he drew closer, he looked back to see Michael pulling Stondrin. Both flew as a team, boosting their wing speed. Grisson slowed down until his velocity matched the power glowing beside him.

"Excellent job, Grisson." Michael and Stondrin panted as they drew abreast of the little angel. "How'd you happen to find it so quickly?"

Grisson shrugged. "It's funny. I felt drawn to it, as if . . . as if God were directing me."

His two companions looked at each other but said nothing.

"Now that we're here, what's next?" the little angel asked.

"I thought someone might be able to throw the power into the black hole and see what happens," Stondrin suggested. "Remember that message from God while we were on the Ledge? It commanded me not to touch the Well of Power. And I got another message from Heaven during the battle that I can now share with you. It said I was not even to touch anything that came from the Well. My purpose won't let me do it, but I hoped maybe you, Michael, might have the strength to accomplish it."

The archangel flew beside the power. He looked it up and down. He seemed to pale as the others watched. Finally, he said,

"I received the same messages as you. As much as I want to use this to help defeat Lucifer, my purpose won't allow me to do it." His whole being sagged. "I think all of us received these messages from God. We're doomed if we stoop to using Lucifer's tactics of disobeying God, and we're doomed if we don't."

Before them, the black hole floated, blocking out much of the sky. It seemed to mock them with its unseen depths.

"I don't have a purpose . . . and I didn't receive those messages."

Michael pulled himself out of his reverie to see Grisson reach for the power. "Don't do it, Grisson! You don't know what will happen!"

"This is one time I'm disobeying you, Michael," the little angel retorted. "I don't have a purpose; I, of all the angels, didn't receive those messages. Do you think all that is just a coincidence?" He waited for a response, but none came. "Again, do you think it a coincidence?"

He took a big breath and grabbed the power in both hands. It seemed to sing to him. Grisson longed to thrust his face into the glowing essence and inhale it into the depths of his soul. There, in the center of the power, something awaited him. If he could only see it clearer. He bent his head to get a closer look . . .

.

Power: it awaits my bidding. Beauty: I am nothing compared to what I could become with its help. Change: the entire universe awaits the one who controls it. Take it. Take it. Come . . . take it now . . . come closer

. . .

"Grisson . . . partner . . . my friend."

The words came to him as if from far away. He felt a hand on his shoulder. Grisson looked up to see Stondrin and Michael staring at him, worried expressions on their faces.

"You've been faithful so far," Michael said. "Don't ruin it now."

The little angel without a purpose nodded once. Then,

drawing his arm back, Grisson flung the essence from The Well of Power toward the center of the black hole.

"What's going to happen when the black hole and the divine essence collide?" Strondrin asked.

Michael grabbed both angels and pulled them to him. "I don't know," he said, "but I don't want t be close when it happens!"

CHAPTER THIRTY

"Join hands, quickly. And fly for The Well of Power!" ordered Michael. The three angels formed a flight team that brought them to the Well in but a moment.

"Angels, leave your battle and get behind me!" Michael's shouted command saw angels disengaging to gather behind Michael, between the planet and The Well of Power.

They watched as the glowing essence arched toward the black hole and sank into its center. Nothing happened for a long moment. Then, a huge explosion crashed through that portion of the universe. Sound and light waves buffeted the angels about. They saw Lucifer's followers blown in every direction. A horrible, screeching noise assailed their ears as the creatures came in contact with the waves of light, and Michael raised his head for a moment to risk a look at what had happened.

"No! No! It's not supposed to happen like this!" Michael was just in time to glimpse a writhing, terror-filled Shi'intor flung toward the Well of Power. Their eyes caught one another for a moment, and Michael saw in them desperation and a realization of doom. Then . . . a flash, and Shi'intor – and his dreams of victory and glory – were no more.

The others opened their eyes to a universe filled with light.

Where the black hole had been floated a cloud ringed with pulsating light. At its center, Telsha'in could be seen winging away from a blinded, crippled Lucifer.

"Quickly," the archangel commanded. "Stondrin, get two of the strongest angels and come with me."

Stondrin's eyebrows were at full height. He was curious about the next move. But, to his credit, he asked not a word. Instead, he pulled two large, stocky angels from the ranks and indicated they should follow Michael.

The four angels headed straight into the brightest part of the light. They seemed to grow stronger as the beams flowed in and around them.

"Telsha'in, sing for us." Michael smiled at the choirmaster as they passed him.

A horrible croak sounded from the former singer. "There is a price to be paid for saying no to Lucifer," Telsha'in whispered. Then he smiled, in spite of the lost voice and the pain. "But I did say no."

The four arrowed down toward the once-mighty Lucifer. He cringed and writhed about, trying to escape the omnipresent light. "Stondrin and I will grab his wings," Michael instructed. "You two take his legs. When I say 'Now,' throw him into The Well of Power. Even Lucifer cannot exist in the middle of such an environment." Michael's voice rang with exultation. The end of this horrible nightmare seemed close, now.

They grabbed the master of evil with ease. Lucifer's strength had dissipated as the light increased. Swiftly, they carried their captive out of the cloud and ever closer to the Well. A roar of triumph rose from the waiting angels. Their faithfulness in the face of what had looked like sure defeat might finally be rewarded.

Creatures scattered toward the planet below. They tried to hide behind mountains, rocks, and volcanoes. The angels let them go for the moment. They knew that without their leader, the monsters could not hope to prevail.

For his part, Grisson gazed in disbelief at what his action had accomplished. He'd thought his lack of purpose to be a difficult burden to carry. Now, in hindsight, he realized God had planned this all along. He bowed his head. "Lord, wherever you are, I promise never to doubt you again. Thank you for Your love."

The four angels flew above The Well of Power. "Drop him!" came the command. Four pair of hands let go. Lucifer fell toward his destruction.

The angels began singing . . . and stopped.

Grisson watched as they raised their heads as one and listed to a Voice he could not hear. With a yell of triumph, they disappeared. At the same moment, the light went out of the universe once more.

With the return of darkness came Lucifer's power and eyesight. In a feat of incredible strength and agility, he twisted at the last moment, put out a hand to touch the side of The Well of Power and used it to vault over and past his intended tomb.

The creatures of evil also gave a roar as they reveled in the new-found darkness. From their earthly hiding places, they converged on the Well and their leader.

Grisson found himself cold, in darkness and truly alone.

Lucifer turned his foul gaze upon the little angel. "Welcome,," he said in a polite tone that surprised Grisson. "I see your God has rejected you, too."

CHAPTER THIRTY-ONE

"Wh . . what are you talking about?" Grisson stuttered.

The creatures of evil and darkness drew closer to him. Lucifer gave him a shrewd glance. "Don't you understand? You must have done something that displeased God. He's awfully unfair, don't you think?"

The little angel didn't know what to think. His mind seemed to be filled with mud that clogged his ability to reason. A moment ago, everything had been wonderful. Then . . .

"All I wanted was power," Lucifer explained. "God wouldn't let me have it." His face twisted in anger. "I could have served Him in my own way if He'd let me. But, no, God won't let anyone else do what they want. It's all about service to *Him*," he sneered.

"Here's what I can do for you, Grisson. You've always been the smallest angel in Heaven. I'll let you keep your flying ability, but make you almost as large as me. You'll be my number two man. Unlimited power and honor can be yours." He dipped his hand into the Well. "What do you say?"

Never again to see the River of Light! Even in the cold vacuum of space, Grisson felt a glow of warmth as waves of light sparkled in his memory. "Heaven," Grisson whispered as he remembered once more.

A harsh voice interrupted his thoughts. "It's time," his captor rasped. "Make your decision."

The angel looked at the creature holding him captive and sighed. "Either choice means I'll never see Heaven again."

The thought of what he'd lost forced tears from his eyes, and Grisson bowed his head in shame.

"Why, God?" he wondered. "Why have You deserted me?"

But raucous laughter from the evil ones encircling him was the only response he received.

A picture of Rendall came floating into Grisson's mind. His teacher had died while trying to tell him something. He visualized the angel giving him his first lesson deep within the cavern on the very light cycle of his *becoming*. It had to do with the River of Light. *"As the light flows all around us, so does God's presence. We can't see Him, but He always sees us. Every time you look at the River of Light, remember this lesson."* Rendall's voice sounded in his mind. The didactic tones caused him to smile in remembrance.

Lucifer saw the smile and thought he'd won. He lifted the power and showed it to Grisson. "Are you ready?"

The power called to Grisson. He remembered how it felt to hold that glowing essence – but he also remembered the joy he felt standing before God's throne and basking in His love. Nothing compared with being in God's presence.

He focused again on the power in the Well. It looked like the River of Light! No wonder it felt so good to hold it. But this belonged exclusively to God, he thought. Neither Lucifer, Grisson, nor any other being had the right to take the power and use it as his own. This light had been created for a special purpose. *"Grisson, as the light flows all around us, so does God's presence."*

Then it hit him. Rendall was partially right, but he hadn't gone far enough. *The seraphim and Lucifer: it's a clue, not a puzzle.*

"Of course!" Grisson spoke aloud. "Lucifer, I have the answers to your puzzle."

Lucifer snorted in surprise. "Where did that come from? Anyway, it's a moot point now. I don't care about Heaven any more."

"Let me give you the answers anyway," Grisson said. "God didn't change the rules. He doesn't allow us to deny our purpose – at least, not without terrible consequences."

The creatures around Lucifer rumbled at this. Lucifer snarled and thrust a fist at them to shut them up. "The seraphim denied his purpose when he left the Throne Room and appeared before me at the barrier," shouted the leader of the fallen angels. "And God did nothing to *him*. God doesn't play fair," the beautiful/horrible Lucifer sneered

"You're wrong again," Grisson said. He swallowed what felt like a lump in his throat and forced himself to look Lucifer square in the eyes. "The seraphim left the Throne Room, yes. But he never denied his purpose because *he never left God's presence*! God allowed all that to happen so we might . . ." Then the realization hit him like one of Lucifer's punches. "God allowed that to happen so *I* might understand, right now, in this moment, that God is everywhere. Not just where the River of Light flows, but everywhere – in the mists, in the Throne Room, at the barrier . . . and right here with us." His eyes glistened with tears of understanding. "God provided this for me thousands of light cycles ago when He sent His seraphim to you. Even then, He knew this moment would come and I would need this strength."

God was here! The light, the Well, the seraphim, all spoke of God's presence! Though Grisson could not see Him, he knew the One who loved him and created him watched and understood everything he'd been undergoing.

Grisson drew a deep breath.

"Lucifer, I don't know why God left me here with you. But I don't think He deserted me. I've discovered that even when we can't understand everything that happens, God is still in control."

He raised his eyes to look square into evil's eyes. "I reject you. I remember God's love for me. I will be found faithful . . ." Grisson swallowed hard. "Faithful to the very end."

Lucifer's face twisted as he listened to the little angel's words. "If that's your decision, and there's nothing I can do to dissuade you, then you're free to return to Heaven."

Grisson could hardly believe his ears. "You're letting me go?"

"Of course," said the new Father of Lies. "After all, the war is over. God has shown He cannot defeat me. The universe is mine to do with as I wish. There's no more hard feelings, little angel. Go your way."

He leaned down toward Grisson. "Just one more thing. As a sign of my sincerity . . . ."

His lips brushed the little angel's cheek. "My friend," he breathed.

Grisson gasped as he felt his body weaken. He looked down to see it growing pale, even translucent. He vowed not to scream, but the pain became too great. Twisting his head, he tried to see the silver portal that led into the Eternal Country he would never see again. But Lucifer blocked his vision.

The pain became intolerable. His vision clouded. Darkness surrounded him.

And Heaven's last angel *unbecame*.

CHAPTER THIRTY-TWO

"The universe is *mine*!" Grunts and rasps of assent greeted Lucifer's proclamation.

The self-proclaimed master of the universe motioned for his minions to gather on the ruined planet beneath them. Now completely black, the planet shuddered as huge chunks of it were torn off and flung into space. Its increasingly erratic orbit and rotation threatened to soon destroy the planet. Oblivious to the destruction, Lucifer strutted before his creatures with pride.

"We won! *I* beat God and his forces. Nothing can stop me now from growing more powerful." He gestured at The Well of Power glowing palely far above them. The monsters he'd created wanted nothing at all to do with it. Lucifer didn't mind at all. Now the Well, and the infinite power it contained, were his alone.

"I will be like God!" he bragged to his audience of fallen angels. "And one day, after consuming enough power, I will rid eternity of Him and His accursed angels."

The yells and grunts began again. Powerful creatures, ready to do his bidding, bowed low before Lucifer. The future lay before him dark with promise!

Above them all, the portal into Heaven closed quietly. And with a "Snap!" The Well of Power disappeared.

CHAPTER THIRTY-THREE

Light. Everywhere.

This first thought came swimming into Grisson's mind. It seemed familiar . . . then he remembered. He'd had the same thought upon *becoming*. Then a second thought followed.

I'm still alive?

"Of course you're alive. You don't think God would ever abandon us, do you?"

I must have spoken out loud and didn't realize it.

"You're still speaking out loud! Quit embarrassing me. I've taught you better than that."

Grisson rolled over and looked up into a face peering at him from only inches away. As the face pulled back, he could see hair going everywhere.

"Rendall!" Grisson jumped up and hugged his grinning teacher. "I thought I'd never see you again." Tears flowed down his cheeks and he hugged his teacher tighter. "I was so proud of you," he whispered. "You paid a high price to stay faithful to God."

Then Grisson frowned as a realization hit him. "But, how can you be here? You were *uncreated*. And . . . why am I here? What . . . what's going on?"

He looked around. A familiar stocky figure stood not far away, showing a rare smile. "Stavros!" Standing beside him, the angel who had befriended Grisson held out a hand of welcome. "*Michael*!" Upon seeing his partner, the fatigue and stress from battling darkness and evil dropped from him like an old, ragged set of clothes no longer needed. The archangel clapped him on the back and turned Grisson around.

Other figures began crowding into the little angel's vision. "Stondrin! LeSage! Toldin and Fradyn! All of us are still alive! And Benla'al . . . you look wonderful!" He ran back and forth to each one of them. Grisson knew he looked silly hugging everyone, but for once, he didn't care what anyone thought. As he continued to take in his surroundings, he saw that all the angels had gathered around – all who had chosen to stand against Lucifer. There were the cherubim and seraphim flying around the Throne . . . . The *Throne?*

God. He was in the presence of God.

Grisson fell to his knees before his Creator. "God, I remembered. I remembered Your love."

"Rise, Grisson." Was that a *grin* on LeSage's face?

"All of you, listen to this message from God." Every head turned to look at God, even as they continued to listen to LeSage. "Our God and Creator is pleased with every angel in this Throne Room. You – we – faced Evil and remained faithful. Though none of us knew it, God was with us every moment. He saw our struggles; He felt our defeats; He watched, in pain, our *unbecoming*."

Then the omnipotent, omniscient God smiled in benediction as LeSage said, "But God is greater than any creature's *unbecoming*. He has created us to live for eternity. And no one, not even the poor, fallen Lucifer, can change that."

"But God, why did You allow this to happen?" Michael, the archangel, seemed surprised to hear the words come from his lips and knelt in confusion.

"Michael!" The grin was back on LeSage's face. "Keep asking questions like that, and we will have to rename you 'Stondrin.'"

All of Heaven resounded with the laughter of victorious angels. Stondrin, for his part, turned a bright red, but kept grinning the whole time.

"The Lord wants us to remember that He designated this the Second Age," LeSage continued. "He also warned us that we would not know its name until we had completed our participation in it. That time has now come. God has named this the *Age of Decision*. For us, it is over. For Humankind, it is just beginning.

"Against great odds, God says we have all chosen to be faithful. None can stand before the Lord for eternity," explained LeSage, "who have not stood against evil and accepted His love. In sadness, I say that some have chosen, forever, to turn their back on Heaven. Those fallen angels preferred what they saw as immediate power and safety. They refused to trust in God's love."

In wonder, LeSage continued. "Angels, God says we have done well! Now, the time has come for our reward."

Grisson saw Heaven's choirmaster take a step toward the Throne. He felt sorry for Telsha'in. To love music as he had, and yet lose his voice . . . .

"Sing, Telsha'in!"

God's command, communicated by LeSage, startled Grisson out of his reverie. He saw that Telsha'in wore a puzzled look, as well, but the angel obeyed. He opened his mouth and tried to follow his Lord's instructions.

Telsha'in's voice startled everyone.

The sound was different from that of the old Telsha'in. No croak or rasp issued from the angel's lips. Instead, the most beautiful, haunting melody ever heard in Heaven wafted up before Grisson and the other angels. Heaven's choirmaster knelt in gratitude at God's gift, even as he continued to sing His praises with a voice far better than he'd had before the Testing.

In the beautiful atmosphere of Heaven, surrounded by God's

love and Telsha'in's finest music, miracles began to happen. As Grisson watched, the angels changed in every way imaginable. Each grew to an enormous height. Their strength increased as well, making the smallest of them as strong as the biggest of Lucifer's creatures. But most of all, the glow Grisson beheld emanating from each of them filled him with awe. These beings of light, in their former guise, were but pale copies of the strong, brilliant angels now standing before God.

One of them, however, outshone all the rest. Michael towered above everyone. The archangel had changed far more than any of the others. His strength and height made him unquestionably the mightiest angel in all of creation.

Glad shouts of triumph filled the throne room of Heaven. Angels marveled at the changes in one another. With great joy, Michael gestured to the other angels to bow down before their God. As he looked around to ensure his order had been seen and understood, his eyes fell on Grisson. He ran a hand through his hair in frustration at the little angel's state. For of all the angels in Heaven, only Grisson remained unchanged.

Already the smallest, this new re-creation of the angels made him so small, in comparison, that Grisson knew he could no longer have a meaningful role in Heaven. Somehow, he must have displeased God. Tears fell on the throne room's floor as Grisson knelt before God in shame.

"Grisson." LeSage spoke gently to the little angel. "You, above anyone else, have performed with great courage."

Grisson looked up, startled.

"Created last, with little training and almost no friends, most of the angels thought you were handicapped by also having no purpose. You only came to God's throne room twice; you spoke with the Lord but once. And yet, you refused to turn from Him. You did not give in to bitterness over having no purpose. Instead, Grisson, you turned what some saw as a weakness into a blessing and a strength. Your courageous use of 'no purpose' to hurl power into the black hole saved the lives of thousands and thousands of angels, and defeated Lucifer.”

“But Lord . . . .” Grisson tried to keep the hurt from his voice, but it bled through anyway. “What about how I look now? How can I be of help in this size and shape?” He heard mutters of assent from the other angels, as well. They knew his tiny size would be useless!

God cast His gaze over the assembled angels and nodded once more to His spokesman. “Grisson will never change in size. Nor will he ever have a purpose.”

Then the All-loving, Omnipotent Creator raised His hand as LeSage said, “Therefore, God will give Grisson a new name!”

A wave of vertigo swept over Grisson. His skin split down the back. A hot beam of light bathed every part of his being and, for a moment, he could see nothing. The little angel stumbled and fell against Michael. To his surprise, the archangel fell down as well. That shouldn’t happen! Grisson carried no weight at all in relation to his mighty friend.

A Divine Hand reached down and raised up the two angels. Grisson looked from his God to Michael – then he looked again. He and Michael were the same height!

“Your name is no longer Grisson.”

LeSage’s voice boomed throughout the Eternal Country. **“I present to you Gabriel. He will be God’s spokesman to Humankind on Earth. Together, Gabriel and Michael will command Heaven’s angels.”**

“Hail, Gabriel,” the angels responded in the timeless ritual. “We praise our God who brought you into being.”

Gabriel looked at the smiling faces surrounding him. He was still unused to his height and strength. A hand clapped him hard on the back, but he never budged.

“Well, partner, it looks like your ‘outside’ is now the same size as your heart and courage.” Michael shook his head in admiration. “If you can still fly as fast as before, I think we’ll do some serious damage to Lucifer and his forces.”

The once-small, spindly angel looked up into the face of his God. "You knew all along of this possibility, didn't You," he whispered. "You wanted to bless me, but I had to go through the Testing first."

The Lord nodded. "You have learned a divine principle, Gabriel," stated LeSage. "If Humankind is to succeed, they will have to learn the same lesson."

"Looking back now," the newly created angel said, "I can truthfully say it's been worth it all. Thank you, Lord, for helping me to remain faithful."

Gabriel stepped back to Michael's side. "Maybe you'll have a more effective partner from now on."

The archangel's close-cropped hair hardly moved as he shook his head. "God always knows what He's doing. I had – and have – the very best partner anyone could hope for."

Gabriel lowered his head for a moment. He noticed absently the floor of Heaven seemed farther away now than when he'd been Grisson. Things were changing rapidly again, and all this would take some getting used to! Then he smiled. These types of changes were a pleasant problem.

"Angels!"

Everyone knelt in response to LeSage's call to honor God. His Love washed over and through them. It left the angels invigorated and joyous. "God says we have many battles ahead of us with Lucifer and the fallen angels. But always remember this: in the end, the victory belongs to God!"

"But why don't you just destroy Lucifer and be done with it?"

Gabriel and Michael chuckled as one. Stondrin had waited as long as possible, but he just couldn't stand it!

"Even Lucifer and the others serve God's purpose in their defiance," responded LeSage. "They will help all Humankind decide who wants to stand for the Lord and who doesn't. For you, *The Age of Decision* is over. For the future inhabitants of Earth, *The Age of Humans* and *The Age of Decision* are just getting ready to begin."

LeSage dropped his voice. "The Lord says that all of us will suffer pain and hardship from time to time. But so will He . . . and far more than any of us can imagine."

Then the voice of God's spokesman rose once again. "But in the end, the joy you have will be greater than you can even envision at this moment. God promises us, the best is yet to come!"

God waved a hand, and the angels found themselves beside the Mists of Light. The silver portal hung before them. "We have one more job to do before Humankind can be created," LeSage thundered over the sound of the mists. "God says it is time to send the fallen angels to their new home."

A golden trumpet appeared in Gabriel's hand.

"Gabriel, sound your trumpet!" came the command.

The powerful angel raised the instrument to his lips and sounded the call. As one, the angels disappeared.

CHAPTER THIRTY-FOUR

The angels appeared without warning in the place only recently occupied by The Well of Power. Gabriel watched as Lucifer rallied his troops for what he thought would be yet another battle.

"Form up!" the fallen angel snarled. "The cowards attack without warning."

This time, however, the monsters seemed reluctant to obey their master. Above them flew huge, brightly glowing beings much stronger than they.

"Come on! What are you waiting for? They might be bigger, now, but you can still send them out of existence!"

And still the creatures hesitated. One or two in the back of the pack began edging their way toward the dubious shelter of the far side of the Earth.

"Come back and fight!" Lucifer yelled. No one, however, listened. Most continued to stare in fear at their changed opponents. Finally, in rage, Lucifer *uncreated* one of the creatures trying to flee.

"Follow me!" he snarled at the rest. "You'll either fight or *unbecome*."

One of his followers, braver than the rest, voiced the thought on everyone's mind. "We can't stand against such strength. Any one of them can throw us into The Well of Power. We're doomed!"

Lucifer ground his teeth in frustration. "Are you all brainless *and* spineless? They can't hurt you, you fools! The Well of Power is gone! They have no weapon to stop us!"

The words had a galvanizing effect on Lucifer's troops. As one, the fallen angels turned from their flight and began organizing themselves. Without the ability of the angels to *uncreate* them, the creatures' shallow courage surfaced once more. Claws unsheathed; heads lowered to point horns toward the heavenly enemy; boldness grew.

"This is not a battle!"

The words came from everywhere.

"There will be no more fighting in this Age!"

Both angels and monsters paused before the mighty power of God as LeSage delivered his Lord's commands.

Lucifer remained unbowed. "Afraid to show yourself, God?" he sneered. "Afraid of my power and ability?"

"Behold your new home, Lucifer."

Below them all, a deep, dark pit revealed itself. Terrible swirling currents of darkness moaned as they clashed against one another and were drawn deep into the bottomless distance. Lucifer's army cried out in terror. They rushed to huddle as close to their leader as possible.

"Your unfaithfulness to God and your greed for power have bought you this place. Now, GO!"

With an insane gurgle, Lucifer launched himself at the first massive angel confronting him. Instead of defending himself, however, the celestial being raised a trumpet to his lips and blew. The sound stopped Lucifer in his tracks. It deafened his army and slammed them backwards. Many of his stronger creatures fought against the sound. The monsters who used to be angels wept as they struggled to stay in place. They raised their hands in supplication and pleaded for mercy. All efforts availed nothing. Screaming horribly, the creatures of evil were pushed over the steep edge and down, down into the Bottomless Pit, until they disappeared from sight.

Lucifer found himself alone with two angels.

Everyone, both his army and the other angels, had departed -- but in two vastly different directions. He peered up into the face of the angel not holding the trumpet.

"Michael?" he ventured. "Is that you?"

The archangel nodded solemnly.

"You've changed. Grown bigger and stronger." He smirked with pride. "But not as strong as me."

Lucifer looked at the other angel, standing just as tall as Michael, and looking as muscular and solid.

"Who are you?" he asked. "God swore He'd finished creating angels, so I must have met you before." He paused for an instant, then . . . "You look familiar, but I don't remember fighting against you."

"My name is Gabriel," the angel said. "You once knew me as Grisson."

Lucifer's eyes grew large as he looked at the figure before him. "How could this be?"

"With God, all things are possible."

Gabriel's cold gaze made the master of lies shudder. "I have taken your place. Because of your pride and lust for power, you have lost everything. I now serve God as His spokesman to Humankind."

Silver seemed to shoot from his eyes as he stared at Lucifer. "We are eternal enemies, you and I. And know this: we, the forces of Heaven, *will* win!"

Lucifer began to hurl an insult, but stopped. He realized he had no one to talk to. The two mighty angels, like the others, had disappeared. For the first time in all of creation, Lucifer found himself truly alone. For a moment, he stared back at the enormity of what had been lost – but only for a moment. He'd discovered it easier to hate than to reason.

"You are no longer Lucifer."

"God?" Lucifer fought to keep himself calm. It was LeSage's voice, but Lucifer knew for Whom he spoke. To remember his former Lord and their relationship! It made his heart ache for what used to be.

"Your new name is now Satan – Father of Lies."

"I reject that name. I prefer to call myself Lucifer."

"Call yourself anything you wish. Everyone in Heaven and on Earth will know you as Satan. You care not for the truth. And in calling yourself Lucifer, you lie even to yourself."

Satan needed a change of subject. He didn't like talking about his true character. "Where is The Well of Power?" he asked. "God never lies. So tell me, will I see it ever again?"

Silence.

Then . . . **"The Well of Power will be a part of your future."**

"Perhaps all is not lost! I still may win!"

Silence.

Satan listened for God, but heard nothing. He now dwelt alone in the darkness.

The fallen angel of angels looked toward the Bottomless Pit. Somewhere within its depths lay his army. He turned toward the terrible blackness. Even if he had to personally carry each one of them out of the Pit, he would not give up. After all . . .

This was war.

CHAPTER THIRTY-FIVE

With a burst of celestial music and Gabriel's accompanying trumpet, God re-enters the universe. Gathered around Him, transformed angels await with eagerness His next act of creation.

From the throne room, God watches with pleasure. In the universe itself, God makes ready to undo and repair the effects of Satan's evil. Below the angels, God hovers over the planet Earth as a mother hen broods protectively over her young.

Gabriel and Michael fly at the heads of the two vast companies of angels. They stand ready to follow wherever their Lord leads them. These angels' Testing behind them, the future holds exciting possibilities.

God thunders with authority, "**Let there be light!**"

The universe obeys, filling with light as it had once before.

The Son creates the sun.

The wonderful story of Divine Love begins.

Mark Sutton, founder of Mark Sutton Ministries, has worked as a full time minister for more than 40 years. He and his wife, Donna, have 5 children and currently live in central Florida, where Mark teaches pastors and church leaders, both in Florida and in Haiti. Mark is the author of 5 books, more than 200 articles, and is currently putting the finishing touches on 2 Christian novels.

For more information on Mark's Haiti minister go to www.marksuttonministries.org.